Wrecked

Studs in Spurs

Cat Johnson

DEDICATION

To all the readers, bloggers, reviewers and cowboy lovers among you who have stuck with me and this series through the years. Enjoy!

STUDS IN SPURS

Unridden
Bucked
Ride
Hooked
Flanked
Thrown
Champion
Spurred
Wrecked

CHAPTER ONE

CeCe Cole watched the thin stream of milk swirl into the black coffee in the mug. It vanished into the brew, leaving the beverage a weaker shade of black. She let out a huff.

"Maggie!" Her annoyance with her assistant, the situation, and her life in general came across clearly in her tone.

There was nothing worse than bad coffee. Too weak. Too strong. It didn't matter which, because either could ruin a perfectly good morning.

This morning, the steaming liquid in the cup wasn't the problem. Her brand new assistant's inability to follow simple instructions was.

This girl, whose only job was to keep CeCe happy, couldn't even manage to do that.

She'd asked for cream, not milk. Was that too much to ask? It wasn't exactly brain surgery.

Her assistant's incompetence was baffling and extremely trying.

At fifty-one, CeCe Cole had completely reinvented herself. She'd taken an active role in the running of Cole Shock Absorbers.

In her lifetime, she'd gone from being a fashion model

from her teens through her twenties, to a trophy wife for the following two decades, to the owner of one of the largest most recognizable corporations in the automotive industry.

That last major move had been accomplished during what could be considered by some people middle age.

Middle aged. God, how she hated that term.

Finally, the newly hired girl appeared in the doorway of the office. "Yes, Mrs. Cole."

"Maggie, it's *Ms.* Cole. I'm no longer married." It wouldn't even be that if the Cole name didn't come with so much power and recognition in the industry. Even so, a return to her maiden name was very tempting. "And I said half and half for my coffee. This is obviously milk. I can tell just by looking at it."

Coffee with cream and real sugar was CeCe's one indulgence in a life that was filled with low calorie, high fiber, healthy foods and relentless exercise.

"Sorry, Ms. Cole."

"I didn't call you in here for you to apologize. Get me half and half." CeCe held out the pitcher filled with the offending milk toward Maggie, hoping the dissatisfaction showed in her expression.

The girl took the pitcher. "Yes, ma'am."

If it hadn't been the housekeeper's day off, CeCe would have already had her first cup of coffee of the day before she left the house and might be a little more understanding now.

Unfortunately for all of them, Maria was off on Mondays. Moving on with her morning, sans coffee for the moment, CeCe ignored the girl and focused her attention on the computer screen in front of her.

"Same old CeCe." A too familiar male voice brought her attention back to the doorway. "Why don't you just cut the girl a break?"

Her jaw clenched, as it always did in the unwelcome presence of her ex-husband, John Cole.

CeCe lifted one brow. "Why? Did you fuck her too?"

It was a valid question. John's liaisons during their

marriage had been many and varied.

John swiveled his head to watch the girl's path across the office as she walked toward the kitchenette. He brought his gaze back to CeCe. "Nope. She wasn't here when I was."

An unladylike snort CeCe couldn't control was her first response to her ex-husband's unspoken text. That being if this girl had worked for him while he'd still been in power of the company, he would definitely have fucked her. Or at least tried.

CeCe scowled. "You're a pig."

"May I remind you that what I am or am not is no longer your concern? A pleasure I paid dearly for."

"You're correct about that. You are definitely not my concern, so why are you here?"

"I need your signature." John tossed a paper onto her desk.

She didn't give him the satisfaction of looking at it. "This paperwork should have gone through the lawyers."

He sniffed at her suggestion. "Those lawyers of yours have cost me more than enough money already. It's just the title to the boat, which if you remember, you gave me in the divorce in exchange for the ski house that is worth far more."

Finally, she glanced down at the paper on the desk in front of her. It did look like the title for the boat, but the fact remained the divorce had been messy.

Hell, the marriage had been messy near the end too. She wouldn't put it past her ex to try to salvage some of what he'd lost by tricking her into signing over something that was legally hers. "I'm not signing a thing without council."

"Why not?" He drew his bushy eyebrows low. Had she still been married to him, she'd have had her hairdresser trim those things.

Nowadays, she was more than happy to see John looking like an unkempt vagabond. She hoped his ear hair was growing in extra thick as well.

Her glare met his head on. "Because, John, I don't trust you as far as I can throw you."

"Come on, CeCe. Just sign the damn paper. I'm not trying to fuck you."

That elicited a laugh from her. "No, you stopped being interested in that the last year of our marriage."

She guessed a man of his age couldn't rise to the occasion as often as when he'd been younger. All of the younger girlfriends he kept on the side must have worn him out before he'd gotten home.

He shook his head. "It boggles the mind that even now you're still not happy. You took me for millions. You made me pay for every indiscretion. You have more money and houses and cars than any one person could use in a lifetime. Yet, even after everything, you're still as miserable a person as you always were."

CeCe narrowed her eyes. "Whatever I am, you made me."

He paused before drawing in a breath. "I'll have my lawyer contact yours about that title."

"You do that." Her retort was far less satisfying than it could have been since he was already out the door and walking away as she had called it after him. CeCe grit her teeth and mumbled, "Stupid, mother fuck—"

"Ms. Cole?"

CeCe halted mid-tirade as she saw another figure darken her doorway—a man she'd never met before to her recollection.

She sighed. "Yes?"

There had been far too many visitors in her office this morning. Especially considering she had yet to drink her first cup of coffee.

Where the hell was Maggie with that half and half?

"I'm Tony Matheson." The older man, sporting an impressively large mustache, stepped forward and handed her a business card.

One glance at the card told CeCe exactly who he was. The knowledge brought a scowl to her face. She tossed the card back down onto the desk. "From the bull riding association. I'm sorry, but I can't help you. I'm no longer affiliated with that organization."

"Yes and no. The sponsorship was paid in advance for the entire season, so technically Cole Shock Absorbers is still the association sponsor until the first of next year.

"Well, if you've run out of money, you can go look elsewhere—"

"It's not about money."

"Then what is it about, Mr.—" CeCe referred to the card again as his name eluded her. "Matheson?"

Maggie finally appeared with the pitcher that hopefully contained the half and half CeCe had requested, but having two distasteful visitors had already ruined her anticipation of her morning cup of coffee.

"We were hoping you'd consider attending this weekend's event."

"Why in the world would I do that?" CeCe leveled her gaze at the man.

She should have realized he'd be bad news from the moment he'd walked in wearing cowboy boots. The last time there'd been a pair of cowboy boots under her bed it had ended badly, to say the least.

If she never attended another bull ride again it would be too soon.

Nope. Not going to happen.

Not after spending the weekend in bed with bull rider Aaron Jordan before he'd dumped her for one of her own employees.

The dead last thing CeCe wanted was to run into Aaron at an event. Or run into her former marketing manager, for that matter. Judging by the way they hadn't been able to keep their eyes off each other, chances were good the two were dating.

Even the mention of the bull riding association brought back memories that gave CeCe a stomachache. Her humiliation thanks to one certain young bull rider was still too fresh.

Nearly a month later, she continued to have a visceral reaction to the topic. It had her pushing her coffee cup away.

"The event is the Cole Shock Absorbers Invitational. It's a tradition for the company's owner to present the buckle to the event winner."

"I guess it's time for a new tradition." She forced a smile she didn't feel.

If there was one thing CeCe Cole was good at it was smiling even when her heart wasn't in it. Especially then. Years of modeling and being in an unhappy marriage had trained her well.

Tony pressed his lips tightly together. "All right. If that's truly your feelings, then I'll take Mr. Cole up on his offer."

That statement piqued her interest. "Mr. Cole's offer?"

The man tipped his head in a nod. "He contacted us to see if we wanted him to make the presentation since he did it last year. And he'll be doing it next year at what I suppose will be renamed the Cole Auto Parts Invitational once his company takes over the sponsorship."

Some of the toughest decisions in life came down to the choice between two evils. CeCe faced that challenge now as she decided which was worse—going and facing the young lover who'd spurned her, or staying away and letting her ex-husband win this round, all while knowing nothing would make the rotten bastard happier.

Finally, the hate and pain of a bitter divorce trumped the emotions of a lover scorned. "Fine. I'll do it."

Tony looked surprised before he recovered his composure. "That's great. Everyone back at the association will be very happy."

"Glad to hear it." Her tone was flat in spite of her words.

"I've taken enough of your time." He turned to go when CeCe panicked.

She didn't know anything about this event named after her company. Certainly not when and where it was being held. "Wait. What day is it? And where?"

"At the arena. The event starts Friday and runs for three days, but the ceremony you'll be presenting at is after Sunday's championship round."

Three days long. The same as the event she'd spent in Aaron's company in Georgia, until he'd crushed her, coincidentally right after Sunday's championship round.

Well, the best revenge was looking fabulous, and she did. She'd come home from that trip and gone directly to her doctor for a little maintenance.

Time did things to a woman, but with some help from modern day science she intended to fight it every step of the way, kicking and screaming.

A few shots for the crow's feet around her eyes, some injections to plump her lips and lift her cheeks, and she felt like a new woman.

Of course, she'd have to go to the hair salon for a touch-up before Sunday, but she had no doubt she looked good enough to make Aaron realize, and regret, what he'd lost.

"I'll leave VIP passes under your name at the ticket booth at the arena. I just need to know how many you'll need."

CeCe remembered the last event she'd attended with someone from the company by her side. It had been that boyfriend-stealing marketing manager Jill.

That bitter memory aside, CeCe had so few moments left in the spotlight at her age there was no way was she bringing anyone with her to steal it.

"Just one ticket is fine. I'll be attending alone."

"All right." Tony nodded. "The opening ceremony starts at two on Sunday. Your ticket for the VIP section will be waiting for you when you arrive."

"Fine. I'll be there." She'd just have to hope that Aaron, Jill and her ex-husband weren't VIPs too. That damn section was too small for them to be in it with her.

She'd also have to hope Maggie was competent enough to find the location of the event. CeCe wasn't about to admit to the man in front of her that she had no clue where this *arena* he kept referring to was. Otherwise, Maggie would have to call the association and find out.

"Have a good day, ma'am."

Only half paying attention as the older man tipped his

head to take his leave, CeCe nodded. "Thank you. You too."

This was no doubt the worst decision she'd made in a long time. At least since her last bad decision of letting herself start to get attached to a bull rider half her age.

Aaron Jordan definitely took the prize as her worst decision of the year.

CHAPTER TWO

"Wade."

The sound cut through the blissful haze of sleep. He ignored it in favor of sinking back into peaceful oblivion for just a little longer.

"Wade."

His name was accompanied by what felt like the toe of a boot nudging him in the ribcage.

"What the fuck? Why're you poking me?" Wade cracked open one eye.

Through the glare of the rider's room fluorescent lights and the haze of sleep, he saw two of the younger bull riders, Aaron Jordan and Garret James.

"You gonna work this event, or you sitting this one out?" Aaron grinned down at him.

"Just taking a little cat nap."

Garret laughed. "Yeah, that's what they all say."

"I'm ready to rock and roll. Don't you worry about it, kid." Wade swung his feet off the narrow wooden bench where he'd been stretched out.

After fifteen years of working protection in the arena as a professional bullfighter, Wade Long knew exactly what he could get away with and still perform at peak capacity.

He also had developed a talent for sleeping anytime and anywhere, no matter how uncomfortable the setting.

Yeah, he had rolled into bed at the hotel after closing time last night, and today was an early start since it was Sunday, but he'd be fine.

No rider was getting hurt on his watch. No fellow bull fighter either. Protection—keeping both riders and bulls safe and healthy—had been his life for too long for him to risk his career for a night out.

But truth be told, after he'd hit forty the aches and pains started to get pretty bad. If having a few shots of whisky after an event to soothe his old battered body helped him sleep at night, then that's what he was going to do.

Now, the two girls who had kept him at the bar until closing and then had waltzed off together, leaving him alone and lonely—that was another story.

They'd been too young for him anyway. He preferred his women to be just that—grown women. Not some girls with the ink barely dry on their driver's licenses.

As Wade was trying to wake up, as well as stand up since his knee was killing him, Aaron's phone buzzed.

The young cowboy glanced down at it. "That's Jill."

"New girlfriend?" Wade asked. Not that he had to. Judging by the way the kid's face lit up just from a text it had to be a girl.

Aaron wobbled his head. "Yeah, kind of. I mean we haven't talked about it officially. Not yet, anyway."

Garret let out a snort. "But he's sure hoping she will be his girl. Especially once she moves to the East Coast. And he did spend the night at her place here in California Friday and last night. You're still paying for half that hotel room, you know. Not my fault you didn't sleep there."

"Fine. Whatever." Aaron rolled his eyes. Wade resisted the urge to do the same.

It must be nice having your only worry be about where to spend the night and with whom. He remembered being young. He hadn't appreciated how good he had it back then. Just like these guys didn't know how good they had it now.

Meanwhile, Wade had an ex-wife and child support payments yanked out of his paychecks monthly for a daughter he saw far too seldom thanks to his life on the road.

That weight on his soul combined with the pain he suspected—when he let himself think about it—was the beginnings of arthritis, didn't help him stand up. He rose off the bench anyway, stifling the groan as he did.

Wade had pulled on his shorts, sponsor jersey and sneakers before his little snooze, so he was ready to work. Bullfighters didn't wear as much equipment as the riders. No mouth guard. No helmet. No spurs or gloves. No chaps or safety vest.

Just man versus beast with not a whole lot in between them. Well, except for that lately Wade's kneepads had turned into knee braces. That was a concession to his body's aches and pains from years of abuse, not a safety concern.

After grabbing his cowboy hat from the end of the bench, Wade planted it on his head and he was good to go.

As he'd promised these two kids, he was ready to rock and roll. "You boys ready for show time?"

"Hell yeah." Garret grinned, his riding rope in his hand.

"Then, let's get." Wade swept a hand for the boys to go ahead of him.

Aaron was too busy texting to answer but he managed to follow Garret out into the hall without walking into any walls.

Wade shook his head at the twenty-something kid. Aaron had succumbed to what was obviously a serious case of young love.

After all these years, Wade knew love was just an illusion brought on by lust.

No need to douse their world in reality. He'd let these boys have their fun now while they were young. They'd learn one day, probably the hard way in a divorce court just like he had.

Fuck, he'd become a cynical bastard.

11

Time to go play with some bulls for a few hours. A good dose of adrenaline generally made everything seem better. Facing off head-on, eye-to-eye, with a massive animal was certain to get the blood flowing.

Wade decided to hit the head before the event started. Rather than follow the two riders out to the chutes, he turned into the bathroom for a quick precautionary pit stop.

Better to go now before the event started even if he really didn't have to piss. He hadn't drunk nearly enough water today to rehydrate after last night's drinking. He'd have to grab a bottle of water.

While washing his hands at the sink, Wade stared at his reflection in the bathroom mirror.

Last night still showed clearly on his face in the dark shadows beneath his bloodshot blue eyes. Even in the way his hair stuck out from beneath his cowboy hat from his nap.

Maybe he'd grab an energy drink instead of that water.

Since the company that made the power drink sponsored some of the riders, there were iced bins of the shit all over. Might as well take advantage of it and replenish the electrolytes he'd lost while overindulging last night at the same time.

Yup, working the pro bull riding circuit was a pretty sweet gig. One he was going to hold on to as long as his body didn't give out. It sure beat working his family ranch on a daily basis like his brother.

Three generations worked the Long family ranch in Texas. Wade was the first and only male to jump ship. That hadn't gone over too well. Not with his dad. Not with his brother.

Gramps tended to live and let live.

At least one family member wasn't on the verge of disowning him for his career choice.

Wade dried his hands and tossed the paper towel in the trash. Now he was ready to hit the arena—or at least as ready as he was going to get.

He pushed through the door of the bathroom and into the hallway, and walked smack into a woman nearly as tall as he was, which was saying something since he was six foot two.

"Whoa, there. Watch where you're going, darlin'." He reached out and grabbed her forearms as the redhead teetered in front of him.

It was no surprise she was a little wobbly, both from their collision and from the insanely high heels she wore.

She lifted one perfectly shaped brow. "I could suggest the same. You walked into me."

Two could play at the attitude game. He raised a brow of his own. "Is that so?"

"Yes, it is." She focused big blue eyes down, staring at where his hands wrapped around her arms.

He liked a woman with some attitude. It made things more interesting.

Amused, Wade dropped his hold on the woman and tipped his hat. "Well then, my apologies, ma'am."

He didn't mention that, in spite of the VIP pass hanging by the lanyard around her slender ivory neck, she was the one who didn't belong in the hallway that led from the riders' area to the arena floor.

Back here was the dressing room and the sports medicine room. She wasn't with the press. He could see that from the pass she wore.

That left the question of who she was—and who she was with. She was probably sleeping with one of the riders or the stock contractors. That would explain the VIP pass and the fact she thought she could barrel down the hallway in a restricted area, but she was older than the typical buckle bunny.

Maybe she wasn't somebody's squeeze after all.

She seemed to accept his apology for bumping into her, when in reality it had been her who'd run into him. Her attitude ratcheted down a notch as she nodded.

"So, is there something or someone I can help you find?" Wade asked.

"No." Her answer didn't answer anything.

She wasn't exactly forthcoming. She sure was pretty

though.

Some men were into tits, others were into asses, but long legs were Wade's downfall and the lovely lady had them in spades. Mile long legs that he couldn't help but imagine wrapped around him.

"All righty then." Wade crossed his arms and waited, wondering what she'd do next since she hadn't admitted to having somewhere to go or anyone to see.

She frowned. "What are you doing?"

Wade lifted one shoulder. "Waiting for you to go wherever it is you're going. I wouldn't want to get in your way again." Her scowl was adorable. It inspired him to extend his right hand in her direction. "I'm Wade."

She cocked a brow and glanced at his hand but didn't shake it. Finally he gave up and pulled his arm back. He should be calling her every name in the book, or at least thinking them.

Instead, the damn woman and her bitchy attitude was getting him hard.

Why was that? Maybe because he suspected such a hard exterior on a woman must be protecting something worthwhile beneath it.

Or maybe he was just into abuse.

More likely, it was because one look told him this woman was like an unbroken horse—wild, untamed and guaranteed to give him one hell of a ride.

He never had been able to resist a challenge.

If nothing else, he could tell this woman would be just that—challenging.

"Wade!" The summons had him turning toward the opposite end of the hallway. He saw one of the other bull fighters wave him over. "Come on. They want an interview before the start."

"On my way." Wade turned back to the mysterious woman. "Enjoy the event."

"Wait."

He paused. "Yeah?"

"Is there an exit through here?" She tipped her head toward the other end of the hall.

"Yeah. There's a fire door down that way. It's where some of the guys who smoke hang around outside."

"Where does it lead?"

"The back lot." Every one of her strange queries piqued Wade's interest a little more.

"Okay." Clutching the bag on her shoulder, she pivoted on one high heel and headed down the hall without so much as a thank you or fuck off.

That left Wade with no answers, but a heap of questions. He watched her ass as she walked away and then turned for the other end of the hall. There was work to do.

By the time Wade reached the chutes he saw not a whole lot of business happening amid the riders, but what looked like a whole lotta bullshit.

"This is a nightmare." Aaron ran his hand over his face.

Garret lifted one shoulder. "I guess it was bound to happen eventually, you running into her again. And this is the Cole Shock Absorbers Invitational. What did you expect?"

Wade was about to walk by. He had an interview to give and the reporter was waiting on him. But this little drama playing out was too interesting to walk on by.

The media guy probably only needed him for a quick sound bite, like usual.

They'd record him standing next to one of the bulls in a pen. He'd say how rank the bull was and what he knew about him as a bucker, then they'd be done. The network would run the thirty second segment sometime during the televised event.

They could wait a few minutes. This was far too good to pass up.

"What's up?" he asked.

"Aaron's former lover and his current girl both have VIP passes for the chute seats." Garret grinned, taking too much joy in his brother-in-law's discomfort, in Wade's opinion.

Wade hid his own smile in deference to the poor kid's

misery. "I see how that could be a problem. What're you gonna do about it?"

He had a few suggestions, but he wanted to see what Aaron came up with on his own. Only way for him to learn was to work things out on his own. Shit like this was bound to happen in this business.

"I don't know." Aaron, looking miserable, shook his head.

Garret glanced at the chute seats above them. "It looks like CeCe left so maybe you don't have to worry or do anything."

Aaron shook his head. "No, she couldn't have. When Jill spotted CeCe walking in, she did a little digging. It looks like CeCe is scheduled to do the buckle presentation so there's no way she left. Besides, I'm not sure she's the kind to turn tail and run."

"No, she's probably not. Damn. You know this'll be the one event you actually win. Then you'll have to have *her* give you the buckle."

Sadist that he was, Wade decided he'd like to see that. At the same time, Aaron groaned. "Great. Thanks. You probably cursed me."

"Hell, it's a damn nice purse. If you win, the money will help you deal with the buckle presentation. Believe me." Garret snorted.

Wade watched the back and forth between the two riders wondering who this CeCe was besides, obviously, somehow part of Cole Shocks and Aaron's former squeeze.

But the reality was, Wade couldn't be all that concerned about Aaron's woes. He had an interview to get to. "Well, good luck with your little problem."

"Thanks." Aaron rolled his eyes and Garret laughed as, chuckling, Wade headed for the media booth.

CHAPTER THREE

CeCe pushed through the exit door and into the sunlight. Only when the door slammed behind her did she feel as if she could breathe again.

Coming to this event had been a monumentally bad idea. She'd suspected that as she started to feel sick to her stomach on the drive over in the limo. She sure as hell knew it for a fact now as she stood outside the back door of the arena not even caring the door had slammed, most likely locking her out of the building.

Of course Aaron Jordan was there. He was a rider. This was a bull riding event. That wasn't a surprise. And Jill was there too, which shouldn't have been a shock at all because CeCe had been assuming all along they'd be together.

What had been a real shocker was how seeing both of them again affected her. She was shaking and angry, sad and hurt all over again.

Weeks afterward and still CeCe felt transported right back to that day in Georgia when Aaron had dumped her and ridden off into the sunset with her marketing manager.

She shouldn't feel like this. She'd spent two nights with Aaron. Only two. But those nights had been when she'd been feeling at her lowest.

The stress of the divorce and her new position as the head of Cole Shocks had gotten to her. Depressed. Insecure. Unsure of the future—her own and that of this multi-billion dollar company she'd gotten in the divorce.

She'd been vulnerable and Aaron had seemed like a port in the storm. An escape from the horrors of reality.

That was the only way she could explain her thinking she was falling for him in so short a time while knowing he was young and that an age difference as great as theirs would present a challenge for the long term in any relationship.

Maybe she needed to take a long hiatus from all men until she got her life together.

Then again, maybe she needed a bottle of booze and a man to make her forget everything, including how her life had gotten so complicated at a time when she should be completely settled.

Who knew what the hell she should do. She obviously was still up in the air.

CeCe leaned back against the wall and closed her eyes, tipping her head back so the warmth of the sun hit her face. For this one moment at least, it felt as if the heat and light could chase away the shadows deep inside her soul.

Then the moment was over.

The door next to her flung open and slammed against the wall too close to her face for comfort. She took a step to one side, as angry about having her peace disturbed as she was about almost being hit with the heavy metal door.

She frowned at the man who walked through.

Recognizing him immediately, she planted her hands on her hips. "Did you follow me out here?"

The man who'd introduced himself inside as Wade widened his eyes. "Follow you? Yeah, sure. Because, you know, I got nothing better to do half an hour before the opening other than stalk you. Jesus. You need a reality check, woman."

Shaking his head, he strode off toward the rows of parked

vehicles in the lot. She watched as he stopped at a big truck. Reaching inside, he grabbed something, slammed the door and turned. Before she'd decided how to respond to his rudeness, he was headed back in her direction.

When he was close enough, he held up a small round can. "See. Just getting another can of chew out of my truck. Not stalking you."

His harsh tone hit her harder than it should have. To CeCe's horror, she felt the prick of tears behind her eyes. "I'm sorry."

"Well, that's good since you're wrong and all." He paused. "What the hell? Hey, don't cry about it."

"I'm not crying. And certainly not about you." She angled her head so he wouldn't see she was lying.

He let out a snort. "I don't know shit about a lot of things, but I know tears when I see them."

CeCe flicked away the incriminating dampness from her eyes. She didn't want to give this cocky cowboy the satisfaction of seeing it. "Don't you have anything better to do?"

"Actually, I do." Still, he didn't go.

She shot him a glare. "Then feel free to go do it."

"I think I'll hang out here for a bit."

She drew down her brows in a frown, in spite of the numbing effects of the Botox injections in her forehead. "Why?"

"Not often I see a wildcat around these parts." The bastard had the gall to grin at her as he leaned back and crossed his arms, settling in. Proof he meant what he'd said and he wasn't going anywhere soon.

"Then I'll leave." Her attempt at finding peace back there had failed.

If nothing else, this man had given her something other than Aaron and Jill to focus on. He'd raised her anger, which had shoved the sadness down inside. For that, she should feel grateful to him. She didn't. She was too annoyed.

CeCe reached for the door handle, praying the door

wouldn't be locked. She yanked it hard and thankfully it swung open. She didn't know what she would have done if she'd been locked outside with the most obnoxious cowboy on earth and his can of chew.

She moved through the doorway, relieved to be making her escape from his unwelcome company until she heard the slow steady sound of footsteps behind her.

Halting, she spun and glared at the man following her down the hall. She planted her hands on her hips and was about to accuse him, or at least question him as to why he insisted on being wherever she was, when he held up both hands in a defensive gesture.

"I'm not following you. I swear." When she looked at him with doubt, he continued, "Really. I gotta get back to the arena floor before the opening ceremony and this is the quickest way to get there. That's all."

That might all be perfectly true, but he didn't have to look so amused about it.

"Fine." CeCe spun back again and strode down the hall.

She realized she was headed directly for the very thing she'd run from just moments ago.

The difference now was that she was fueled with a nice dose of anger thanks to this infuriating Wade person.

Let Aaron or Jill dare say anything to her. She'd take them on and anyone else who got in her way.

"CeCe!"

Ready to fight the world, she pivoted in the direction of the summons. She saw Tom Parsons, the head of the bull riding association, stepping out of a doorway and tried to take her agitation down a notch. But if he had anything negative to say about her pulling the Cole Shock Absorbers' corporate sponsorship for next year, she'd give him a piece of her mind.

"Yes?" She forced a smile in return to the one he wore as he strode toward her.

He extended a hand to shake hers. "I'm so happy you could make it today. It really means a lot to the association to have a member of Cole Shocks present the buckle."

She didn't get why but she nodded and pretended she did. "My pleasure."

"I see you got the VIP pass. Do you need me to show you to your seats? The show's about to start."

"Actually, regarding my seat—" She nearly didn't say anything but hell, as long as he was kissing her ass she might as well take advantage of it. It would make today a lot easier to deal with. "I was wondering if I could talk to you about that."

"Hey, boss."

She and Tom had stood there long enough, Wade, Mr. Annoying, had caught up with them.

Tom took a step back to include the cowboy in their conversation. "Wade, have you met CeCe Cole? She's here representing Cole Shocks today for the Invitational. She'll be presenting the buckle."

CeCe took a modicum of pleasure watching his eyes widen at the revelation.

"Uh, not officially introduced, no. Ms. Cole. A pleasure." His eyes never leaving hers, Wade tipped his hat.

It was a move that looked so practiced she would have assumed it was all for show for the attendees if she hadn't already heard him speak. That heavy southern drawl wasn't fake. Neither was his good ol' boy pick-up truck or the can of chewing tobacco in his grasp.

Though that he wore sneakers instead of boots seemed odd to her. Very anti-cowboy, in her opinion, but what did she know? She tried not to think about cowboys or their boots since the debacle with Aaron.

Tom turned his attention to her again. "Wade Long is one of our bullfighters."

"Like in Spain?" she asked.

Wade cocked a brow at that, but let Tom answer the question. "No, ma'am. They're the men who distract the bulls to make sure the riders get out of the arena safely after a match-up."

"Ah." Feeling mean, she cast a glance at Wade and added,

"So you're basically like human shields, then."

In spite of her verbal slap, he grinned wide and looked as if he really meant it.

"Yup. You could say that." He let out a snort. "That's a pretty accurate description actually."

She hated when a well-crafted insult fell flat. But he certainly was intriguing. It seemed the more she tried to piss him off, the more he enjoyed it. As if her verbal sparring got him going.

Then again, a man who threw himself in front of charging bulls for a living probably had some issues, mentally.

"I'm sorry. You were about to say something before about your seat. Is it not acceptable?" Tom asked.

Wade, who clearly didn't need to be here any longer, still remained. Short of asking him to leave her and Tom alone, she had no other choice but to just ignore him.

"I was wondering if there was someplace else I could be during the event." She directed the inquiry to Tom, but noticed Wade listening as intently as if she'd talked to him.

"But the chute seats are the best we've got." Tom looked distressed and baffled that she was unhappy.

His obvious concern should have made CeCe feel better about the whole situation. Usually people scurrying to keep her happy gave her great satisfaction. But really, right now all she wanted was someplace to hide until she had to give away that damn buckle and she could leave.

Someplace far away from Aaron and Jill.

"I understand. And I appreciate that. But—"

The loud ringing of Tom's cell phone interrupted CeCe. He glanced at the read out and cringed. "I'm so sorry but I have to take this. Wait right here and we'll figure this out about your seat."

"Fine." She nodded and watched as he moved farther down the hall to take the call.

Unfortunately, Wade didn't make a move to leave. He remained right where he was, looking amused.

She scowled at his mere presence. "I thought you had

somewhere to be."

"I do. I'll get there. Why? You worried about me?" He grinned.

"No." She said it with conviction so there'd be no doubt in his mind. All that seemed to do was amuse him further.

"So, CeCe Cole of Cole Shock Absorbers. I'll be damned."

Could it be that *finally* he was impressed with her? Maybe now he'd show her some respect. Although from what little she knew of him from their short association, probably not.

She crossed her arms. "Yes. And? That surprises you?"

He bobbed his head. "A little bit. Yeah. But it also explains a whole hell of a lot. On the other hand, it raises a few more questions too."

"Well, sadly for you, you'll have to live with those questions. It looks like Tom's done with his call so if you'll excuse me, Mr. Long."

He grinned even as she brushed him off. "Ain't nobody calls me Mr. Long. You can feel free to call me Wade."

"I seriously doubt I'll have occasion to call you anything, but if in future I do I'll keep that in mind." She spun on one high heel and moved to meet Tom as he walked toward her.

She heard Wade snicker behind her and her blood pressure rose.

Damn, stupid, obnoxious man.

How did he have the uncanny ability to get to her so easily?

The bigger question was, why did she let him?

That was a question she could ponder later, perhaps as she watched the crazy man throw himself in the path of a charging bull.

Right now, she had to figure out where she was going to sit so she wouldn't have to see Aaron and Jill. If not, she might be inspired to throw one or both of them in front of a bull herself.

CHAPTER FOUR

"Are you sure you don't want to sit closer?" Tom Parsons looked concerned, which had become a familiar expression for him it seemed, ever since CeCe had told him she didn't like the VIP seat he'd put her in.

"I'm sure. This is fine. Thank you."

He hesitated again. "If you change your mind—"

"I promise I'll let you know."

Finally, Tom nodded. "All right. I need to check on some things but I'll be back to look in on you later."

"Okay." Jeez. If her ex-husband had been half as attentive as the corporate executive kissing her ass, she might still be married.

Then again, Tom Parsons had the association's coffers to worry about. He was probably hoping she'd change her mind about sponsorship for next year.

Who knew? Maybe she would change her mind. It would piss off John to no end and that was worth any amount of money.

Pissing off the ex—priceless.

CeCe's cell phone rang. One glance at the display had her rolling her eyes.

It was John.

Speak of the devil.

Had she somehow cursed herself by just thinking his name?

She touched the screen to answer. "Yes, John."

"Where are you?" he asked.

He had a lot of nerve. He'd lost the right to ask her that question in the divorce, right along with a considerable part of his fortune. That's the chance he took when he decided to partake of pleasures with other women during their marriage.

She decided she wasn't going to make this call any easier for him. "Why? Where are you?"

"Dammit, woman. Can't you just answer a simple question?" The frustration was clear in his voice.

Of course she could answer his question, but what fun was there in that? "You answer me first and then I'll answer you."

"Fine. I'm at the arena."

That bastard was trying to steal her spotlight. Well, he had wasted his time. Come hell or high water—or bull manure, as the case may be—she was doing the buckle presentation. Not him.

CeCe had been intent on playing with him for longer, but that was not to be. The announcer's amplified voice bounced off the walls even as loud music began to pound from the sound system. Most likely John would be able to hear she was also at the arena, if he hadn't figured that out already.

She sighed and gave in to the fact her game was over. "I'm at the arena too."

"Where are you? I'm in the VIP section and I don't see you."

"That's because Tom Parsons got me a better seat." Not quite the truth, but CeCe figured John didn't need to know any more than that.

"Oh."

She didn't have long to enjoy his envy over her supposedly *better* seats before John continued, "Are you going to present the buckle or do you want me to just do it?"

Ah ha. Exactly as she'd suspected. He wanted to be the one to stand in the middle of the arena amid spotlights and cheers.

This presentation was still officially hers to do and she intended to do it. "Yes, I'm going to present the buckle. Alone. So don't get any ideas."

"I'm not. I just wanted to make sure. You do have a habit of leaving the association in a lurch, you know. Can't blame them for wanting to have me here as back up."

Rotten bastard. Throwing in her face the fact she'd pulled next year's sponsorship. She couldn't argue it was true but John had plenty of faults of his own for her to mention.

"And you have a habit of cheating so what's your point?" It wasn't the best insult she'd ever come up with, but she didn't have much time to think and the noise level in there was nearly deafening. She functioned better in quiet. "Listen, John, do us both a favor and stay away from me today. Enjoy the show and your VIP seats. Oh and make sure you say hello to my *former* marketing manager Jill for me."

She hung up before she could second guess that last comment about Jill.

That bruise was still fresh. It would take a while for CeCe to stop feeling the twinge of knowing Aaron had chosen Jill over her.

Stupid, fickle bull rider. Men nowadays really had no clue.

The action on the arena floor drew her attention away from her sorrows. She wasn't all that knowledgeable or interested in this sport, but she was here so she might as well watch and try to make the best of it.

The lights dimmed and CeCe braced herself for what she knew was to come. She might not be a professional fan such as her husband, make that ex-husband, but it had only taken her one event to know that the opening ceremony was overly loud and explosive—literally.

The producers in charge of the association's events certainly loved their pyrotechnics. They used enough explosions to fill the arena with smoke and even flames. CeCe wouldn't be surprised if the bright flashes and deafening bangs were enough to induce seizures.

Over the top. That described these events in a nutshell.

Modern day bull riding had become a commercial business. And the professional bull riding organization was a marketing machine. She knew personally how much money it took to run these events that were becoming more of a show than a competition.

The announcer began introducing the riders. CeCe staunchly tried to not listen, to ignore Aaron's introduction, but that was impossible. As the announcer's words reverberated off the walls of the arena, they hit her doubly hard.

There were a lot of riders and even reading off the names at a fast clip it took a while to get through them all. Then they moved to the other arena personnel.

CeCe had been to all three events that weekend in Georgia, but she had to admit she hadn't paid all that much attention to anything except Aaron. Besides, Jill was there distracting her as well.

Today, CeCe was alone and becoming a little bored.

"Bullfighter Wade Long—"

With nothing else to pay attention to but the action down on the arena floor, CeCe couldn't help but notice when the man she kept inexplicably bumping into was introduced.

At the sound of his name on the loudspeaker, Wade came trotting into the arena waving to the crowd along the way.

Given the sideshow atmosphere, she was surprised an older man like Wade would willingly be a part of it.

Guys like Aaron, flighty and young, fit right in here. But Wade? Not so much. Not that she knew much more about the cowboy than what she'd observed during their couple of encounters.

She knew that he chewed tobacco, just like she remembered her grandfather doing when she was little. She knew he drove a ridiculously huge, good ol' boy truck and that he had the attitude to match.

He ran around the edge of the arena wearing long shorts, obnoxiously bright sneakers and an oversized shirt with none other than the Cole Shock Absorbers' name and logo emblazoned across the front and back.

That mind-boggling ensemble was topped off by a cowboy hat. In comparison to the basketball shorts and crazy sneakers, the hat looked as out of place on his head as the man himself looked in the arena amid the dozens of others clad in jeans and leather.

CeCe pushed her fashion critique of the bullfighters aside as the actual bull riding began.

Compared to the lengthy opening, which included a prayer, a presentation of the flag and the national anthem, the competition itself moved fast.

That was the one good thing about bull riding. If nothing else, it didn't drag on. So much better than the golf tournaments John used to watch.

She'd endured more than enough hours of watching men chase a tiny white ball amid hushed whispers and golf claps. Or worse, hours of watching cars drive in a circle during those races John loved so much.

In contrast, watching bull riding was a pleasure.

The first rider and bull charged into the arena before the scent of the smoke from the opening had cleared.

According to the announcer, the bull was Captain Hook, but CeCe missed the name of the bull rider. Not that she cared all that much. The only rider she knew from among the three dozen plus was Aaron anyway. She could see it wasn't him riding.

Nope, she could see Aaron clearly, standing directly below the VIP area she'd wisely chosen to opt against sitting in.

At about the same time that a loud buzzer sounded, the rider was launched off the back of the bull and landed face down in the dirt.

Three men, Wade among them, circled the bull. They deflected the spinning animal's attention from the downed rider and for the first time since meeting him, CeCe finally understood Wade's purpose in this event.

Bullfighters, they were called? More like bull magnets as they waved their arms and in some cases, hats, in front of the animal to attract its attention away from the fallen rider who was still vulnerable.

The bull took the bait. It lowered its head and charged straight at Wade. As she watched, wide-eyed, he sidestepped the direct assault at the last second.

This job seemed almost as insane to her as actually riding the bull did. Having met him, and seeing him now laughing and joking with the other men, she figured he was just nuts enough to enjoy it.

It felt like barely a minute later the next gate swung open. There was a flurry of activity as a new bull and rider shot into the arena.

Without having had time to even catch his breath, Wade was by the bull's side. Along with his fellow bullfighters, they surrounded the animal, waving their arms at him and shouting.

"Why do the bullfighters circle the bull like that? Wouldn't it be better to stand out of its way?" CeCe wasn't one to talk to strangers usually, but the question poked at her and she wanted to know the answer.

The woman next to her didn't take her eyes off the action as she said, "It's to keep the bull bucking in a tight spin."

"Oh." CeCe turned toward her, about to ask next why the bullfighters wanted the bull to stay in a tight spin, when the woman sucked in a breath.

CeCe's focus whipped to the action on the dirt. She saw the reason for the woman's gasp immediately.

The rider had slipped off but remained attached at the hand as the bull kept bucking. The rider tried to stay on his feet even as he was flipped around like a rag doll by the powerful animal's motion.

He was going to get trampled. There was no way around it.

CeCe's heart seemed to stop beating as she watched the horror unfold before her. "Why doesn't he let go?"

"He's hung up." When all CeCe did was frown at the woman, she continued, "His hand. It's stuck in his rope."

"Oh my God." That information had CeCe's eyes widening as she watched.

Wade ran alongside, grabbing for the rope that bound the rider to the deadly bull.

The animal didn't take kindly to Wade's attempt to help. Just as the rider fell to the ground, finally free of the rope binding him, the bull turned its giant head toward Wade and flipped him up into the air.

Like a gymnast, Wade spun in a complete circle while airborne before crashing flat on his back in the dirt.

CeCe covered her mouth. She could only imagine what that fall had felt like, but what was worse was that now Wade was on the ground just feet from where the bull's four hooves pounded with deadly force.

Things moved so quickly she could barely track the motion. A man on a horse somehow got a rope around the bull's neck while the other two bullfighters ran to the downed rider and Wade.

Seconds later, more people ran into the arena, males and females who didn't look like bull riders or the organization's suited executive staff.

"Who are they?" she asked.

"Sports medicine."

Was there no real medical crew on site? From what she'd seen of this sport, there should be a full team of EMTs and an ambulance inside the damn arena.

CeCe intended to find out why there wasn't and then demand they include one for future events. She paid a fortune to sponsor this deadly sport. No men were going to die because of it if she had any say in the matter that could prevent it.

So many people surrounded each of the men she couldn't see them. Her panic increased until a cheer erupted through the arena that had become deadly silent as the crowd held its collective breath and waited.

"He's up." The woman next to her pointed in the direction where Wade had fallen.

Sure enough, he stood and lifted an arm to the crowd to prove he was fine. One of the guys handed him his hat and he planted it back on his head as another cheer sounded.

"The rider's up too."

At the woman's announcement, CeCe swung her gaze and saw the rider limping out of the arena with the help of two of the medical professionals.

She'd spent three days sitting in the VIP seats during the events in Georgia but apparently she hadn't paid all that much attention to the action, because she didn't remember seeing anything like this.

CeCe blew out a breath. "This sport is insane."

The woman sitting next to CeCe sent her a sideways glance. "Welcome to bull riding."

CHAPTER FIVE

"Hey, Clint. Let me ask you something."

The stock handler, who had been watching the same award ceremony play out on the dirt that Wade had been, glanced over. "Sure. Ask away."

"What do you know about this CeCe Cole?" Wade followed CeCe's progress as she picked her way across the arena floor in heels not meant for dirt.

Tom Parsons assisted her progress with a hand on her arm, leading her toward the winner of the event for the buckle presentation.

Wade had been piecing together the many parts of this mystery all event. The details were slowly falling into place in his mind like pieces of a partially completed puzzle.

CeCe Cole's strange behavior today, including the tears. Her choosing to sit way up in the media box rather than in the much closer chute seats. Aaron Jordan's fear about his ex and his current girl being here at the same time and running into each other. Garret James's many snarky comments on the whole thing.

But in spite of what Wade knew, and what he'd guessed, this particular puzzle still had a whole lot of holes left to be filled in. For one, what the hell had a sophisticated, mature, rich as Rockefeller female corporate executive been doing with Aaron Jordan in the first place?

Clint lifted one shoulder in response to Wade's question. "What do I know about her besides the fact that she's hot as hell, you mean?"

Wade lifted a brow. "Yeah. Besides that." A detail he hadn't missed himself.

"I don't know a lot besides that something happened last month that threw a wrench in the whole Cole Shock Absorbers' sponsorship."

"Really?" Wade frowned. He hadn't heard anything about that. Then again, he generally kept his head down, doing his job and leaving. "What happened?"

Given this event was the Cole Shock Absorbers Invitational and CeCe was here, and the bullfighters and the riders all still had the Cole Shocks logo on their vests, it seemed like not all that much had changed.

"I don't know exact details, but I heard the head guys at the association totally freaked out about Cole Shocks pulling out for next year's sponsorship, but then Cole Auto Parts stepped in with a big old check to make up the money."

"Huh. Maybe it was some sort of corporate bullshit? They had to juggle it around for the accounting." It could all be a ploy to shelter profits from the IRS. Who knew what problems these super rich folk had? Certainly not Wade.

"I think it had something to do with the Coles's divorce. It was supposedly pretty messy, personally and corporate-wise. She got one part of the company and he got the other."

A messy divorce. Now *that* Wade could understand. He'd gone through losing half of everything he owned, plus some.

What Clint was saying made sense though. A bad break-up would explain CeCe's tears and her bitch attitude.

Hell, it could even explain what a woman like CeCe Cole had been doing with a mediocre bull rider half her age.

The presentation went off without a hitch, playing out on the arena floor in front of the cameras and the live audience.

CeCe presented the buckle and the check to the winner, a rookie Brazilian rider not that much older than Wade's own kid. It seemed the riders got younger every damn year.

Luckily for Aaron, it turned out he didn't have to worry about the awkwardness of facing CeCe for the presentation. He hadn't even placed in the money, so there was no chance he could have won the event.

The kid had ridden like shit. He hadn't even covered his ride today.

Bull riding was as much mental as it was physical. A man had to have his head in this game or pay the price for it.

After all these years, Wade could see from across the arena when a rider was distracted. Inevitably, those were the riders he ended up having to drag out of the bull's path once they hit the dirt long before the clock showed eight seconds.

Clint let out a low whistle and shook his head. "I tell you what, though, I wouldn't want to be in her ex-husband's shoes. I bet she's one tough bitch. Of course, I wouldn't mind a taste or two for a night."

"Yup, I hear ya." Having been on the receiving end of CeCe's verbal claws himself, Wade had to agree with Clint's evaluation of her bitchy attitude.

He tracked her progress back across the arena and had to agree with the other part of Clint's statement as well. The woman was a walking, talking wet dream.

Her short tight skirt showed off long creamy thighs and hugged hips he wouldn't mind wrapping his hands around.

A go-round with CeCe Cole would surely be nice and definitely far from boring.

He tore his attention off his sexual fantasies. The stands were beginning to empty. "That's it. Time to wrap up and go."

Clint snorted. "You mean you can go. There's still stock I gotta load."

"Then you'd better get to it." Wade grinned, not feeling guilty. His job was done for the night and he had fresh bruises and dirt covering him to prove it. "See you next week."

As he turned to head to the dressing room, Clint called after him, "You heading home for the week?"

"Maybe. Haven't really decided yet. Talk to you later." Wade lifted one arm in a wave goodbye and kept walking.

Home. That was another thing in Wade's life, in addition to his failed marriage, that hadn't worked out quite as he'd planned.

Going home to the family ranch between events always caused too much emotional shit he'd rather not deal with.

The black sheep of the family, returning home, only to leave again a couple of days later—all it did was create unnecessary upheaval in everyone's lives.

Fuck it. Maybe he wouldn't go home.

A good bullfighter could always pick up work. There could be some local rodeos happening mid-week near here, or close to next weekend's event venue.

It was something to think about—later. Now he had to clean up and change.

Following that, an adult beverage and a few hours to wind down at the bar near his hotel would definitely be in order.

And after watching the smoldering hot CeCe Cole all night, if a nice piece of tail happened to land in Wade's lap, he wouldn't say no to that either.

Maybe fifteen minutes later Wade had washed up, changed and was ready to go. Clean jeans, boots and a clean collared shirt were as good as it was going to get unless he went back to his hotel room.

He wasn't all that worried. He'd been to the bar last night and knew even like this he'd likely be overdressed. Half the males in the place were in T-shirts or tank tops, some of them not even all that clean.

It looked like some of them had come straight from work and hadn't bothered to change.

Bag in his hand, Wade headed out to his truck in the parking lot where he saw that, even with as quick as he'd been, he'd taken too long.

There was a line of vehicles waiting to get out as he swung his truck into the queue. He waved his thanks to the driver who'd left an opening for him.

If the bar was just a little closer, he'd leave the damn truck here and walk. But hiking a mile wasn't what he felt like doing after an event. Not with sore ribs from taking a horn to the back from Mad Man and the twinge in his ankle from twisting it as he sidestepped to get out of the path of Redneck Romeo.

Sad he knew the bulls and their names better than he knew some of the riders.

Of course, he tended to like animals better than people most times.

Sighing, Wade shoved a fresh pinch of chew between his cheek and gum. He'd just settled in for a long wait to get out of the lot when he spotted a long black car parked along the curb.

And lo and behold, who was heading toward it but CeCe Cole herself.

Of course she'd have a limo. Why not? She had the bucks. He really shouldn't be surprised. And as luck would have it, he was inching past the car just as she reached the curb and the driver holding the door open for her.

Wade rolled down his window. "Hey! Nice ride."

She raised her gaze to meet his. "Thank you. Nice, uh, truck."

He grinned. "Hell yeah, it is. Top of the line. King cab. Leather seats. The works. Why don't you hop on in and I'll take you for a ride."

Oh, yeah. He'd like to take her for a nice long ride, all right.

She lifted one reddish brow. "Um, thanks but I'm good in the limo."

He'd bet she'd be good in the limo. Hell, she'd be good anywhere. "Well, if you change your mind, I'll be just down the road at the bar next to the Homeside Inn."

While sending him a look that said pretty clearly he should keep dreaming, CeCe did him the favor of saying, "Have a good night."

She disappeared into the limo, probably never to be seen again—at least by his eyes.

Oh, well. At least that had been a diversion while he waited.

As the light to exit the arena lot turned green, a space opened up between him and the car ahead. Feeling generous, Wade waited and let the limo pull in front of him before he made his slow and steady way to the exit.

Wade noticed CeCe's limo turned left, while he turned right toward the hotel and bar.

His brief brush with auto parts royalty was over. It had been fun while it lasted.

He hit the accelerator and sped up to highway speed. A cold beer and warm whisky were waiting on him.

CHAPTER SIX

CeCe watched the scenery from behind the tinted windows of the limousine. With every mile that passed her restlessness grew until she was ready to jump out of the car even as they sped down the California highway.

By the time the driver pulled through the soaring metal gates of the home she used to share with her husband she was itching to get out.

The house and property were for sale and if it ever sold in this market the proceeds would be split between her and John. She could have chosen to keep it and pay him for his half, but giving that man anything after he'd cheated on her ate at her gut.

Besides, it was better she make a fresh start in a place of her own. Maybe a nice secluded beach house where the waves could lull her to sleep. Or a penthouse in some city where she would always be surrounded by people and excitement and never have to feel alone.

Alone. That's what she was in this mausoleum of a house, since the house and grounds staff only came for a few hours a day on weekdays.

The driver parked and, leaving the engine idling, came to

open her door.

She stepped out onto the cobblestone circular drive. "Thank you."

"Yes, ma'am." He tipped his head and then got back into the car.

As the red taillights glowed in the evening light while he pulled out of the driveway, CeCe turned back to the house.

As grand as it was, it was far from being a home—and she realized she didn't want to be there.

Rather than go inside, not even to change, she turned toward the carriage house-turned-garage. She punched in the key code to unlock the door. Inside she reached into the cabinet and grabbed the keys to her convertible from one of the hooks inside.

She hadn't driven it all summer. It had been too damn hot so she'd chosen the sedan and air conditioning.

Today, she wanted that feeling of the wind in her hair. The feeling of freedom that came with the sports car.

On the highway, she punched the accelerator and pushed the car well past the speed limit. For the first time that day, she felt like she could really breathe freely.

She realized her craving for an idle drive had her heading back the way she'd come.

Not long after that, she passed the arena.

Passing the entrance she remembered Wade's invitation to the bar next to his hotel.

Where had it said it was? Just a mile or so away?

She saw a hotel and next to it a building sporting the telltale neon that indicated a bar was within.

What the hell she thought she was doing she didn't know, but she slowed the car as she neared. Then she swung off the road and into the parking lot, creeping between the rows of parked vehicles.

The lot was packed, but one truck stuck out amid the rest. She recognized that truck. If she wasn't mistaken, it was Wade's and he was inside.

He was probably dancing with some young thing wearing

a tank top and cut-off shorts with cowboy boots right now.

And if he was? What did she care? She didn't. She was simply restless and looking for a distraction.

The music pumping loud enough inside that she could feel the bass all the way outside in the car should provide just that—a distraction from her lonely life.

Hell, maybe she'd even order a beer. Or maybe a bourbon. Or both. Isn't that the kind of things people drank at honky-tonks?

CeCe didn't really know. By the time she'd turned legal to drink in most states in the United States she was already earning in the high six figures annually and modeling internationally.

Needless to say, she didn't hang out at these kinds of places then. Her pre-marriage years were spent flying between Manhattan, Milan and Paris. No cowboy joints there.

Then, after marrying John, she went where he took her. The Ritz. The Carlyle. The Beverly Hilton. The same places he took his mistresses, which is how it was so easy to catch him.

Creature of habit, that man.

The point was, John Cole might like to pretend he was a good ol' boy at times, going to car races and sponsoring bull riding events, but he also had massive amounts of money and he spent it accordingly. No falling down buildings housing a local watering hole for him, which is what made this place pretty perfect for her night of escape.

No memories of the past.

Resolved, she pulled into an open spot that seemed big enough the car wasn't in danger of being smashed into by any drunks getting into one of these huge trucks.

After running a hand through her windblown hair, and deciding by her reflection in the rearview mirror that she looked pretty good, she got out.

She should drive the car more often. It gave her color in her cheeks and her hair a kind of tousled, sexy look. She'd probably fit right in here. She could only imagine there were plenty of women inside looking rumpled from all the physical attention they were getting from cowboys such as Wade.

There were a few people standing around outside the exit smoking since that wasn't allowed inside. The two men followed CeCe's path with their eyes while the one woman sent her an interested glance.

Perhaps she was overdressed for the venue, but she never had been one to tone things down.

As she pushed through the door into the dimly lit space, she looked around.

Wade hadn't been among the people outside smoking. Not a surprise since she'd seen for herself he chewed tobacco.

Nope, Wade was inside and she saw him now. He stood at the bar and the expression on his face when he saw her enter was priceless.

The bottle in his hand poised halfway to his mouth, he lifted his brows before smiling.

He took a sip and then pushed away from the bar, sauntering across the floor as casually as if he had all the time in the world to reach his destination—her.

"Well, well, well. Look who's here. Miss Cole Shock Absorbers, herself."

"Actually, the only official title I held was Miss South Carolina but that was many, many years ago."

"You? South Carolina?" He shook his head. "You don't sound like it."

"Thank you." She appreciated the compliment more than he could know. She'd worked long and hard to rid herself of any regional accent whatsoever.

"So, what made you change your mind about joining me? My charm?"

"No. Definitely not." She smiled sweetly and it wasn't even fake.

The banter between them was the most entertaining conversation she'd had with a man—hell, with anyone—in ages.

Employees pandered to her. The lawyers talked down to her. Those in a service position, from masseuses to maids, barely talked to her at all. But this, with Wade, was actually fun.

"Ah, so then you decided to go slumming for the night. And this is the perfect place for it, I can tell you that." He glanced around them. "Let me help you get the full experience. There's an empty booth over there. Come sit down with me and have a drink."

"Me? Sit with you? That's presumptuous of you, no?"

"Not at all. I just figured until you've sat in a sticky booth in a dark corner and enjoyed the atmospheric fragrance of beer and vomit, you haven't gotten your money's worth."

"I haven't spent any money yet."

"That's easily remedied. Jolie!" he shouted in the direction of the bar.

A waitress carrying a tray and baring a good amount of cleavage turned at the summons. "What ya need, darlin'?"

"Two beers and two shots. We'll be in the booth." He hooked his thumb in the direction of the empty table before he turned his attention back to CeCe. "There you go. All taken care of. You can have the pleasure of buying me a drink."

"Do women usually buy your drinks? I thought it would be the other way around. You buying women drinks to get them drunk so they'll go home with you." She allowed him to lead her to the table.

She slid into the booth first taking note he was correct about the atmosphere. It was both dark and fragrant and not in a good way.

He sat next to her and shook his head. "Nope. Now see, you're wrong there."

"Am I?" She added a good bit of doubt in her tone.

"Yup. I don't usually take them home with me. Too hard to get them out again afterward." He grinned and she couldn't help but smile at his crude joke, in spite of herself.

Jolie planting a glass on the table startled CeCe. She didn't get service this fast at some of the best restaurants.

One look at the smile Jolie sent Wade, as well as how she bent over extra low to deliver his drinks, told CeCe why they were getting such star treatment.

"Wait. Let me get out my wallet." CeCe reached for her purse on the table.

Wade frowned at her. "I was only kidding about that. Jolie, put it on my tab."

"You got it, darlin'." The woman, who was a good ten years older than CeCe had first assumed now that she'd seen her close up, winked at Wade before she turned away.

"She a friend of yours?"

"Friend? No. But it was a three day event and this place is right next to my hotel so I guess I've spent about as much time with her here as I have spent lately with some I do call friends." He raised the shot glass in one hand. "To Cole Shock Absorbers."

Surprised at his proposed toast, CeCe raised her own shot glass in the air and then pressed it to her lips. The amber liquid burned a path down her throat, making her choke. She reached for the beer and chugged a big swallow. "What was that?"

"Jamieson's." He looked at her strangely. "You struck me as the type to be able to handle her whisky."

"I can."

"A'ight. If you say so." He hid his grin behind his beer.

She drew her brows down at the insult. "I can hold my liquor. I'm just not in the habit of doing shots of whisky."

"Ah, yes. More the martini type, are you?" he asked.

"Actually, yes. Dirty Martinis to be precise."

"Dirty, huh? I like the sound of that. I'll have to try me one of those one day."

"You should. They're excellent."

"That may be, but it's not gonna be tonight. I think it's safest to stick to beer and shots at this place."

She glanced at the kid behind the bar, who might not be old enough to drink legally himself. "I think you're right."

"Can I ask you something?"

"Only if I can ask you something in return."

He looked surprised. "Okay. It's a deal."

"Fine. Ask your question." CeCe took another gulp of her beer. It was so cold she found it went down like water. Fast and smooth.

Wade noticed her draining her glass and held up two fingers to the waitress before he turned to CeCe. "Okay, here's my question. Aaron Jordan?"

Those two words had her eyes widening, before her blood pressure shot high. "He told you?"

"No. Calm down, beautiful. He didn't. I overheard Garret James mention your name in regards to Aaron. I wasn't inclined to believe him until just now when you confirmed it."

There was no use lying about it so CeCe lifted one shoulder. "Temporary insanity."

"It must have been. He's a kid."

"So you're saying I'm too old to be with him?" She planted her palms on the table, ready to stand up and leave. If Wade didn't have her blocked in the booth, she would be gone already.

"No. Don't get your panties in a twist. I'm saying he's too young to be with you."

"That's the same thing." She scowled at his supposed logic.

He planted his hand over hers, holding her in place. "No, it's not. A woman like you needs a man, not a boy. You would have been bored with him inside of a week. You need a strong man and a strong hand."

CeCe noticed he hadn't moved his hand off hers, even when the waitress appeared with not just two beers, but two more shots.

Even Jolie noticed. She glanced down at Wade's big hand covering CeCe's before she yanked her gaze away.

"Thanks, Jolie." Wade finally removed his hold on her to lift the shot glass. "To a strong hand."

She wasn't sure she agreed with that toast, but she didn't argue and did the shot anyway. It seemed she was full of bad choices lately. Might as well add tonight to the list.

"My question now. Did you have sex with her?" CeCe tipped her head toward Jolie, now standing at the bar.

Why she asked that was confusing even to her. She was curious, but underneath that, there was something else completely irrational. Jealousy.

"Who? Jolie?" Wade asked, looking surprised by the question.

"Yes."

"Why? Do you care if I did?"

"That counts as a new question for you to me and you haven't answered mine to you yet."

Wade's lips twitched. "I didn't realize we were keeping track of questions or conquests."

"Stop trying to talk your way out of answering."

"No, I didn't have sex with her."

"Hm." That was a surprise. "Why not? She's obviously interested in you."

"Is she?" He smirked.

"Yes." That much was obvious to CeCe and to Wade too, judging by his expression and his tone of feigned ignorance.

"The God's honest truth is I was planning on it that first night. I figured I'd insure my entertainment for the weekend. She's close, you know location-wise. That would be convenient. And I'd probably get free drinks."

All logical things in a man's mind, CeCe supposed. "And what happened?"

"The bartender on Friday night told me what a rough time Jolie's been having lately. Single mom. Deadbeat husband walked out and isn't paying his support. A woman like that is vulnerable. Easy to hurt. She doesn't need me waltzing into her life for three days and then leaving." He shrugged like it didn't matter all that much.

Kind of blown away by the crack in the smart ass armor, CeCe realized his confession had probably been a bigger revelation about himself than he'd intended to make.

"Wow. That was really decent of you."

"Yeah, sure. And that shock in your voice didn't negate that compliment at all." He shot her a sideways glance ripe with sarcasm.

She cringed. "Sorry. I didn't mean to sound that way."

"Quite all right." He drew in a breath. "My turn again. Why did it matter to you if I had been with her?"

CeCe laughed. "I honestly don't know."

He eyed her for a moment before lifting his beer and taking a sip. "You wanna know what I think?"

"Sure. Go ahead." They were already down the rabbit hole. This night couldn't get much more surreal.

"I think you needed to feel in control. That's why you chose to be with a boy."

They were talking about Aaron again? And he was insulting her too. "He's hardly a boy. He's in his mid-twenties."

"I'm not talking age, beautiful. I'm talking wisdom and experience. At about his age I was married and about to be a father. Not too much later, I was divorced and paying child support." He cocked a brow and paused as CeCe let all that information sink in. "On the other hand, rumor has it Aaron's mamma still does his laundry every week."

So many more revelations about the man and his life. And as he drank another gulp from his glass, it seemed Wade hadn't even realized he'd made them.

He glanced up, caught her looking at him and frowned. "Why're you staring at me like that?"

"You're not what I expected."

"Well, that statement there is ripe with all sorts of shit I don't think I want to hear." He grinned and shook his head.

"You're probably right." She had assumed the worst about him. She wasn't hiding her surprise very well that she hadn't gotten it.

"So why are you here tonight, beautiful?"

"That's a new question."

"You didn't give me a very satisfactory answer to the last one so this one doesn't count."

"Fine. Why am I here? Because I didn't want to be home and I guess I had nowhere else to go." She averted her eyes when she felt those damn tears threatening to rise to the surface again.

What was it about this man that had her wanting to cry all the time? She had to give him credit though. He didn't question. Or comment.

The shock came when he squeezed her hand for the briefest second and then drank some more beer.

She lifted her glass and did the same, realizing she was getting tipsy. "I'm going to be too drunk to drive home anytime soon."

"Hotel's right next door."

"You hitting on me?" she asked.

"No. Actually I was telling you there's vacancies according to the sign out front so you don't have to drive tonight."

"Oh." CeCe didn't know what to make of that.

Was he not interested enough to hit on her? Or worse, had Wade pigeonholed her in the same category as Jolie? Too pitiful to sleep with.

She glanced up to find him watching her closely. "I think you're right."

"About what?" he asked.

Forcing her gaze to hold his, she said, "A boy wasn't what I need."

Wade's eyes narrowed and for the first time he looked completely serious and not one bit amused. "CeCe, don't play with the bull unless you're looking to get stuck by a horn."

She didn't have to be a bull rider to understand what he was saying.

Her being here. Drinking with him. Talking about personal things. Alluding to sex even . . .

Wade was telling her if she wasn't interested in going all the way with this—with him—she'd better back off now.

As much as he joked around, she had a feeling he wasn't

CAT JOHNSON

the type to play games when it came to the serious stuff.

She should be ordering a cup of coffee and maybe some food if they had any. She should sober up and leave. Or get a room, alone, and sleep it off.

Instead all CeCe could think was that Wade probably had a really nice horn and she wouldn't mind being stuck by it. Not one bit.

Definitely too much to drink. She pushed her beer away.

"I see an awful lot of thinking going on in that pretty head of yours, beautiful. You need to know something while you're doing it. I'm not looking for a girlfriend or a wife."

That elicited a snort from her. "That's good because the last thing I want right now is another husband."

He tipped his head. "Fair enough. Then what do you want?"

"To forget."

He watched her for a few seconds more before he nodded. "That I can help you with. Stay here. I'll go settle up the tab."

Wade stood and was gone to the bar before she could second guess her decision and tell him she'd changed her mind.

She was still debating with herself when he returned and extended his hand to her. "Come on. Let's get out of here."

Swallowing hard, CeCe took his hand and slid out of the booth. She was crazy. Or drunk. Or both.

Or maybe Wade was right. She'd needed to forget—her lousy marriage, her cold big empty house, her next birthday looming ominously close before her.

Wade might just be the man to help her forget all that.

"You got everything?"

"Yup." She held up her purse. It held not much more than a cell phone, wallet, lipstick and car keys. She wasn't exactly prepared for a night of sex in a stranger's hotel room.

Then again, she might be overthinking things. Raw simple sex just for the sake of having it really wouldn't require more than what she and Wade had both been born with.

Simple sex. She really liked the idea of that.

CHAPTER SEVEN

"So I have to admit something to you." Wade glanced back at her as they pushed through the exit of the bar.

"What's that?"

"I never had me a redhead and I have to ask, does the carpet match the drapes?" He grinned wide as the crudeness of the question made her gasp.

"You're a pig." She slapped his arm, but couldn't resist answering. "And there is no carpet."

Maybe it was just her attempt to try and shock him, the way he had her.

He glanced sideways, brows raised. "Really?"

"Really."

Wade bobbed his head. "Nice."

"So glad you approve." She followed as he led the way to his truck.

"Oh, I approve." He clicked open the locks and opened the passenger door before turning to lift her onto the seat of the truck. "So let's see."

She held the bottom of her skirt down as Wade planted his palms on her knees and began to move his hands up her legs. "In the parking lot of the bar? Are you crazy?"

"Some have said that, yeah." He'd already started to push her skirt up in spite of her efforts to stop him.

"We can't do this here. What if someone sees?" She glanced around them, hoping the parking lot remained empty of people until she could talk some sense into this man. "What if we get arrested?"

"You said you wanted to forget everything about your life. Well, all those questions you're firing at me will keep you too occupied to think of much else, won't they? That is until I get a chance to distract you properly." He managed to snake his hands up beneath her skirt.

Distracting was the right word as Wade rubbed her through the fabric of her underwear.

"We shouldn't—"

"Wrong. We definitely should." He slipped his finger beneath her underwear and CeCe's breath caught as he made contact with her bare flesh.

When he parted her with one finger, his teasing forced a sound of pleasure from her.

That encouraged him more. He added another finger and doubled the speed with which he worked her. Soon, he added a thumb and she was overwhelmed by the sensations of him filling her channel while rubbing the sensitive bundle of nerves that had her hips tilting toward his touch.

He smiled. "Mm. You're beautiful when you're about to come."

"I'm not going to do that here."

"We'll see about that." He yanked her underwear down, all the way, pulling the lace garment over her shoes and completely off. "Damn, you have got the longest legs of any woman I've ever seen."

The compliment was nice, she supposed, but she wasn't concerned with how he felt about her legs at the moment. There was a far greater concern.

"Wade, don't you have a room we can do this in?" She wasn't past begging he take them somewhere more private. "Or please, at least let me book us a room—"

He stepped in closer between her legs, forcing her to open them wider. "Hush up. And if you can't bring yourself to do that, just wrap these gorgeous legs of yours around my head so I won't have to hear you."

Before she could protest he'd leaned low between her spread thighs. He separated her flesh with his thumbs and his mouth connected with her clit.

She gasped. "Wade. Really, stop. Someone could come—"

He lifted his head just enough to say, "Someone is gonna come all right and it's gonna be you. Lay back, hush up and enjoy."

He yanked her closer to him, which forced her to fall back onto the bench seat, but she wasn't sure she could do what else he asked her to.

She was all for a little bit of exhibitionism, but that had been in the back of her private limo with tinted windows and the privacy glass raised. Not in a bar parking lot in the cab of a truck with the door wide open.

Thank goodness Wade was parked toward the back where the lights didn't reach. Since he'd backed into the spot along the edge of the lot, the open passenger door shielded them a bit from view. Not nearly enough. If anyone walked by to get to any of the many nearby vehicles, they'd be sure to figure out what Wade was doing with CeCe's legs wrapped around his head.

The man was obviously a danger junkie, from his career choice to his sexual recreation.

She was about to tell him that when he pushed his fingers into her while sucking her clit between his lips, working her inside and out.

His mouth was hot and wet, treating her to just the right amount of suction and pressure. His hands were big and strong, the rough skin abrasive where he held onto her one bare hip. The fingers inside her were just as rough as he moved them hard and fast, in and out.

The combination was enough to have her breathing faster.

Amazingly, it was even enough for her to start to not care

where they were or who might see as long as he made her come.

He increased the speed and intensity of his actions and she felt the first wave of the orgasm break over her.

Her muscles clenched around Wade's fingers inside her as her cries filled the interior of the truck.

Her body was still convulsing when he lifted his head. He was breathing as heavily as she was as he said, "I need to fuck you. Now."

He reached for the glove compartment. It popped open next to her.

Before she knew what was happening, he'd opened his belt and jeans. "Wade. Not here—"

"Yes, here." He pulled out his erection from his underwear and rolled on the condom he'd grabbed from inside the dashboard.

Before she had time to convince him that she didn't think full out sex in the parking lot was a good idea he'd slid inside her with one fast thrust.

The force of it drove the breath from her lungs.

Wade clenched his jaw as he stroked in and out of her. He hissed in a breath between his teeth. "God, you feel good."

She hated to admit it, but what he was doing to her felt good too.

So good.

She'd needed this, to be taken, hard and rough.

How he knew that, if he knew that, she didn't know, but he was giving her exactly what she needed.

He must have needed this as much as she did. He didn't last too long. No surprise considering how hard he took her.

In a few minutes he was grunting with every thrust, before he finally drove in hard and held deep.

His back bowed and he let out a groan that anyone within hearing distance would have been able to identify for what it was.

Wade didn't move. He just held inside her, panting, his head dropped forward so his forehead rested against her chest.

She had yet to catch her breath herself when she couldn't wait any longer to chastise him. "Seriously, Wade, why did we have to do this in your truck?"

Wade raised his head and took a step back from her. Horrified, CeCe watched him snap the used condom off and toss it onto the ground. He ignored her reaction and instead grinned and began to right his clothing.

"I'm assuming you came here tonight to experience how the other half lives. So I showed you." He lifted one shoulder.

"As if the cheap hotel right next door wouldn't have been enough of a taste of how the other half lives? We had to have sex in the parking lot instead?"

He tipped his head to the side. "Hey, you should be glad. My truck is a big step up from a stall in the bathroom of the bar. That's as far as some women have gotten when I fucked them."

A frown wrinkled her brow as she began to revaluate her opinion of Wade one more time, back to her initial view that he was just a womanizing pig.

He probably figured he could ditch her faster here than if she'd gone to his room. And she'd played right into his hand and let him have his way with her.

CeCe realized she was staying true to form. Poor decisions, every time.

Wade reached out and smoothed his thumb over her cheek. "Hey. You wanna know why it had to be here?"

"Yes." She couldn't wait to hear this bullshit excuse.

"I couldn't wait. Not one more minute to have you."

She rolled her eyes. "Come on. The hotel is right next door."

"Which means I'd have to get in the truck, drive over there, park. Get out, walk through the damn lobby with a hard-on ain't nobody gonna miss seeing, take the elevator up to my floor where my room is at the end of a very long hallway. And if I remember correctly, I left my room looking like a pigsty. I figured that would be a mood killer for you so .

. .." He shrugged.

He sounded sincere enough. But still, she was having trouble believing him. "You really couldn't wait to have me?"

"Nope. There was a very real chance I would have taken you in the elevator if we had tried to make it to the room. Though I'm sure the night staff watching the security monitors would have enjoyed the show." He leaned in and pressed a kiss to her mouth. Soft. Almost chaste.

Their first kiss. It was odd. They'd fucked. He'd had his mouth in much more personal places tonight, but this kiss felt intimate.

He pulled back far enough to ask, "So do you forgive me?"

"Yes." She'd never had a man want her so badly he couldn't wait even five minutes.

"So, first time having sex in a pick-up truck, I assume?"

Did he really have to ask? She laughed. "Uh, yes."

"Good." He looked particularly satisfied with her answer.

"Why is that good?" she asked, surprised.

"Then you'll always remember it. A girl always remembers her first time." He winked.

"I suppose I will." As if she would ever forget this incredibly strange man, truck sex or not.

Wade reached toward the floorboard and handed her the underwear he'd taken off her. "Put these on and fix your clothes so we can go."

"Where are we going? The hotel?" That figured. Now. After they were done.

"No." He took a step back to give her room to maneuver getting her underwear on in the tight space. "The diner. I'm hungry and I'm betting, judging by the looks of you, you didn't eat tonight."

"What do you mean *the looks of me*?" She was so insulted she stopped with the panties halfway up her legs.

"I mean you're too skinny, woman." Even as he said it, she did notice he hadn't taken his eyes off her legs or the high heels she still wore.

Apparently he wasn't that upset with her being too skinny, judging by the look of appreciation she saw in his eyes.

"I am not too skinny." She finished wiggling into the lace panties and then had to work her tight skirt back down over them.

Wade had sure managed to mess up her clothing fast enough. But it wasn't nearly as fast or easy to put it all right again.

"Yes, you are. You need some meat on those bones and I intend on helping you do that right now. The diner has the best chili cheese fries I've ever had."

"I don't eat chili cheese fries." If she did she certainly wouldn't have maintained the same size figure she'd had since she started modeling in her teens.

"Tonight you do." He slammed her door closed and walked around to the other side of the truck, cutting off her protest until he was inside the cab with her.

"And what makes you think I'll do what you ask?"

He shot her a sideways glance as he slid the key into the ignition. "You have so far."

She wanted to protest but when she thought about it, dammit, he was right. Instead she asked, "Are you okay to drive?"

"Me? Yeah. Besides, the diner is just on the other side of the hotel. I figure I'll move the truck to the hotel lot and we can walk to the diner."

He drove through the back entrance of the bar's lot and directly into the hotel parking spots. From there she could see the lights of the diner next door. Everything a person could ever need—food, drink and a place to sleep—all within a few steps.

This slumming it—as Wade called it—wasn't so bad. But she'd come in a car that probably cost more than Wade's annual salary. "Is it okay to leave my car parked at the bar?"

"Sure. Drunks leave their vehicles overnight at bars all the time but I'll walk over and move it for you later so it's not there all night."

"All night?" She lifted her brow in question.

Safely parked in the spot, he cut the engine and turned to her. "Yup. I'm not nearly done with you yet."

"Oh." That was all CeCe could come up with as he grinned.

In a surprising show of manners, Wade ran around the truck and opened her door for her. Then her hand was in his as he led her next door to the diner.

It was all so surreal all she could do was let him lead the way.

When they walked through the door, one of the waitresses inside barely glanced their direction before telling them to seat themselves anywhere.

With his hand pressed to CeCe's lower back, Wade led them toward a back booth. She slid into one side and to her surprise he slid in right next to her.

CeCe frowned. "You do know there's a whole other side to sit on right over there, right?"

"Yup. But from over there, I can't do this." He settled his hand on her knee.

CeCe had the distinct feeling that Wade's hand wasn't going to stay where it rested now. That it wouldn't be long before he moved it up her leg, beneath her skirt, seeking more. "You are insatiable."

"Only for you, beautiful."

She didn't believe that one bit, but couldn't comment because the waitress was there and looking at them to order.

"Hey, yeah. Coke for me. CeCe?"

"Water, please." She cringed when she realized that the water here would no doubt be from the tap and not imported and in a bottle like she usually drank.

"And to eat?" The waitress stood, poised with a pen and pad in her hands.

"One order of chili cheese fries and a burger. Well done." Wade turned to CeCe. "You?"

"No, I'm good."

The waitress nodded. "I'll be right back with your drinks."

Then she was gone.

Wade shot her a sideways glance. "You're eating some of mine."

"Why? I'm not hungry."

"Sure you are. You just don't know it yet."

She laughed. "How can you know what I am?"

He lifted one shoulder in a casual half-shrug. "You'll see."

Damned if Wade wasn't right. The moment the plates arrived on the table and the aroma of hot fresh food penetrated the air, CeCe's stomach let out a low grumble.

Wade's grin turned into a chuckle. "Told you. Eat."

He pushed the plate closer to her, even as she shook her head. "No, thanks."

"Eat. I'm not going to listen to your stomach growling all night." As Wade focused on the giant burger on the plate in front of him, CeCe took note of his words.

All night.

As she considered the implications of those words, CeCe decided to give in. She'd try one French fry just to make him happy. Hopefully that would prevent him from trying to force the giant burger on her as well.

One fry wouldn't kill her. She popped the hot, salty, deep-fried golden strip dripping in melted cheese into her mouth. The flavor and texture combined in a culinary pleasure that defied logic.

This was greasy diner food yet she wanted more.

When she reached for another fry, Wade shot her a sideways glance.

"It you say *I told you so*, I'm going to dump this plate of fries right in your lap."

Shaking his head, Wade said, "Wasn't going to say a word."

CeCe didn't miss the hint of his smile just visible past the burger he brought up to his mouth.

CHAPTER EIGHT

The elevator door had barely closed when Wade decided he couldn't control himself any longer. He'd been good during their time at the diner. Mainly because he was so happy to see her eating he didn't want to disturb her.

There was no plate of food in front of her now. He pushed CeCe against the back wall and pressed his thigh between her legs. He smashed his mouth against hers at the same time he ground against her.

His belly was full of some damn good food and now it was time to satisfy another pressing need.

Unfortunately, CeCe's fighting him was interfering with his plan and ruining his good time.

"What the fuck, girl? Stop shoving." He grabbed both her hands in one of his and held them above her head.

"We're in the elevator."

"So?"

"Someone could come in." Eyes wide, she whispered it as if this imaginary someone might hear her.

"It's late and it's Sunday. Ain't nobody riding up and down in this hotel this time of night." That's what made it the perfect time to do what he had every intention of doing. He was forty. Time to cross this little item off the bucket list.

Sex in an elevator. Check.

Sex with a hot-as-hell supermodel. Double check.

Who's also a billionaire. That wasn't on the list but he'd add it later just so he could check it off too.

To convince CeCe that she'd enjoy this as much as he would if she'd just let herself, Wade ran his free hand up the bare skin of her leg. He did love a woman in a short skirt. It made things so easy.

Slipping his fingers beneath the lacey edge of her underwear, he worked his way until he hit her wet heat.

The doors slid open, and he pulled his hand back. Breathing hard, he glanced over his shoulder and, just as he expected, all he saw was the empty hallway.

"Isn't this your floor?" She went to move.

He kept her pinned in place blocking her way with his body. "Yup."

"Aren't we getting off?"

He grinned. "Hopefully we'll both get off."

The doors slid closed as she said, "But—"

Wade was on CeCe like a starving dog on a juicy steak, cutting off any further protest. As he worked her mouth with a hard deep kiss, he used both hands to push up her skirt.

She turned her head to break the lip lock. "Wade, we can't."

"Watch me." His belt was already open and he was in the process of pulling out his cock.

He wasn't as crazy as she thought. The elevator hadn't moved since the doors had closed. It remained at the floor where they should have gotten off for his room and hadn't. If anyone called for the elevator, it would most likely be from the lobby. They'd feel it move and be dressed again long before the doors opened and embarrassed them.

CeCe pursed her lips, staring at him unhappily, as if he was a child misbehaving.

Finally, she let out a breath. "Do you have a condom?"

Wade couldn't help his smile as she gave in. "Always."

He bent and unzipped his bag on the floor.

The condoms were right on top where he'd tossed them when he'd taken them out of the glove compartment in the truck.

He was suited up in no time, and then there wasn't a second to waste. He didn't get this close to his schoolboy fantasy of sex in an elevator only to have it ruined by some insomniac who wanted ice from the machine on the first floor.

Wade whipped her underwear down her legs, pulling them off her feet past her shoes. Standing, he shoved the lacey panties in his bag, considering keeping them as a memento of this occasion.

Then there was nothing standing between him and his sole goal—being inside CeCe.

Even after what should have been plenty of notice of what he was about to do, CeCe let out a squeak as he hoisted her up.

"Wrap your legs around me, beautiful."

Bracing her against the wall, he lowered her over his length. He groaned as her heat surrounded him.

He could fuck her sweet pussy all day and all night. And if he ever said that to her, she'd act all offended. Possibly— probably—slap him.

Shocking her was too much fun. He'd consider it for later.

Right now he was too busy thrusting into her and wondering how long before they got caught.

It was the most fun he'd had since—well, since leaving the bar when he'd taken her in the parking lot.

Chili cheese fries . . . Sex in an elevator and in a pick-up truck . . . Shoving a spoiled princess like CeCe Cole so far out of her comfort zone she might never find her way back . . .

It had all proven to be quite an unexpected pleasure and he wasn't finished yet.

He wasn't about to risk getting interrupted by taking too long. Wade pushed himself to completion, pounding into CeCe fast and hard before he got screwed out of finishing.

The power of the blessed release when it came made him weak in the knees. Panting, he eased her feet back down to the floor. She stood with her palms and back pressed against the back wall, breathing heavily.

"Now, we can go." He zipped his jeans quick and then spun to the panel of buttons and punched the number for his floor.

The doors swished open immediately since the elevator hadn't moved since arriving. Though Wade wasn't sure he'd have noticed if it had moved. He bent to grab his bag on the floor and noticed CeCe looking a bit shell shocked as she pushed her skirt back into place.

She hadn't seen anything yet. Wait until he had her in private and in a bed. Then she'd get a real taste of what it was like to be with him.

Lovin' in an elevator had been fun, but he owed CeCe an orgasm, or three given how incredible that experience had been. Wade always paid his debts.

CHAPTER NINE

"Good morning, beautiful."

Morning? It couldn't possibly be morning. It felt as if she'd just fallen asleep.

CeCe groaned. "What time is it?"

"Early." He flung one arm over her and pulled her against him.

"Then why are you awake?" She realized it was a silly question the moment she asked it.

As Wade pressed close behind her, she felt very clearly the long hard reason he was awake.

She cracked one eye open and saw the glow of sunlight filtering through the hotel room curtains. At least he'd waited until after dawn to bother her.

"You're insatiable."

"So you keep saying, but I don't hear any complaints so . . ." He groaned as he ran his palm down her bare leg and then moved his hand between her thighs.

The truth was, she wasn't complaining. It had been a long time since a man had been unable to keep his hands off her.

Even as she felt the soreness in parts of her body John had long neglected during the last years of her marriage, she knew she wouldn't try to stop Wade. Not seriously, anyway.

After a moment of movement and rustling behind her, Wade was back, pressing his length between her legs.

CeCe shook her head on the pillow. "I can't believe you're not out of condoms yet."

"Nope. Buy them in bulk."

"Lovely. That makes me feel really special. Thanks." CeCe scowled.

"You are special." With one well-placed thrust, he was inside her, as if that would prove his point.

She hissed in a breath as the sheer number of times they'd had sex over the past twelve hours caught up with her.

"You okay?"

"I'm a little sore." She heard his chuckle and her spine stiffened. "It's not funny, Wade."

"No, it's not funny. But forgive me if my male pride enjoys it just a tad, okay?" He stroked into her, but more gently than before. "Maybe I can distract you."

Wade's idea of a distraction was a multi-front assault on CeCe's senses. As he drew the lobe of her ear between his teeth, he found her clit with the fingers of one hand. His other hand he slid beneath her and pulling her close he cupped her breast.

One pinch of her nipple between his fingers sent a shockwave of desire shooting through her.

The warmth of his hard body behind her, being encased in his arms as he loved her slowly and gently, was a tantalizing combination. She closed her eyes and let out an open-mouthed breath tinged with a moan.

Wade echoed the sound behind her. "Better?"

"Maybe." Her breath caught in her throat and she thrust her hips forward, seeking more as his fingers between her legs pressed harder.

"Liar." There was the sound of a smile in his voice.

A few well-angled strokes hit a spot inside her that had her body tightening, building toward release.

"Shut up, Wade." She needn't have made the demand. He

was too busy kissing down her neck to speak, but she felt better saying it anyway.

CeCe had to at least pretend she was in control of this situation, even as it was very obvious she wasn't.

Not at all.

The orgasm built, slow and steady, until it reached a crescendo. Only once she was writhing beneath his touch did Wade pound himself to a loud, shaking finish.

He was still buried inside her, both of them breathless, when he said, "I could get used to waking up to this."

So could she. As the tiny voice of reason in her head said no, CeCe said, "Then don't go."

It was stupid. Crazy. She'd never learn. She'd tried to get Aaron to stay with her too and that had been a disaster.

She was good and truly fucked up. John probably deserved some of the blame for that. That didn't make her feel any better as she waited for Wade to blow her off.

"A'ight."

"What?" She twisted in his arms to face him. "All right?"

He lifted one shoulder in a half shrug. "Sure. I can hang around town for a while. I got a few days before I have to leave for the next event. I reckon I could come up with a few ideas on how to occupy that time." He swept her naked body with his gaze before focusing back on her face. "You going to be able to stand this place for a few more nights?"

"No."

"No?" He lifted his brows and laughed. "Then what are you going to do?"

"Go back to my house." There was no need to stay in this place when she had that empty mansion with a king sized bed and Egyptian cotton sheets waiting for her.

"Okay." He dipped his head. "I understand you wanting your own bed. I suppose I can hang out here if I know you'll be stopping by for more of this."

Wade ran his hand up her body, leaving a trail of goose bumps behind.

He obviously had misunderstood her. "Actually, I figured

you'd come with me."

"To your place?" He lifted his brows high.

"Yes."

He hesitated long enough she braced for him to say no. Finally, he bobbed his head. "I guess I could do that."

"Really?"

"Uh, huh. Let me ask you something. This the house you used to live in with your husband?"

"Yes."

"The husband who cheated on you?"

"I've only been married once, so yes."

He nodded again. "Okay."

"Why'd you ask that?"

"Revenge is a powerful motivator. I'm figuring it could make for some pretty kick ass sex."

"Our sex hasn't been *kick ass* already?"

"Oh, it has. Which is why it'll be extra interesting to see where it can go from here." He grinned wide before he delivered a slap to her ass cheek with his open palm hard enough to sting. "Get up. I'm hungry."

She rubbed the tender flesh and frowned. "You're always hungry."

"For one thing or another, yup, that's probably true. But right now, I've got steak and eggs on my mind."

"Steak for breakfast?"

He raised a brow. "You know after a comment like that I'm gonna make you try it."

"I usually just have coffee for breakfast. Sometimes melon."

"There's no protein in any of that. It's no wonder you're so pale I can practically see through you. You got no iron in your blood."

"I am not—"

"Today you're gonna have eggs."

She was finding it was easier to just humor Wade.

Besides, he'd bowed to her request for a few more days and nights of mind erasing sex in the comfort of her own bed. The least she could do was try his stupid steak for breakfast.

"Fine." CeCe drew in a breath and let it out. "Do I have time to shower first?" She felt a little sticky from all the sex.

He grinned, obviously pleased with himself that she'd given in so easily. "Sure. Take all the time you need, beautiful. In fact, I think I'll join you."

She shook her head at his persistence. "Somehow I don't think that's going to save time."

"Nope. But it will be time well spent and a whole lotta fun too. Mm, mm. You all wet and sudsy. I can hardly wait." Wade grabbed her hand and pulled her up and off the bed.

In spite of herself, she had to laugh at his enthusiasm. He might be exactly what she needed to soothe her bruised and battered ego.

Then, maybe, she'd be able to figure out what to do next.

CHAPTER TEN

Wade followed in his truck as CeCe led the way in her car.

They drove from the parking lot of the hotel, down the California highway.

The scenery changed with every mile that passed and though it wasn't all that far, by the time CeCe slowed and flipped on her blinker, they might have been in an entirely different world.

She turned into a drive and pulled slowly through a set of imposing wrought iron gates that had Wade wide eyed as he drove his truck between them. The driveway circled in front of a building bearing an impressive stone façade.

"Damn." He let out a long slow whistle and leaned forward to try and see how far above him the house soared.

CeCe Cole was no bullshit rich. As in billionaire kind of rich, like someone who owned one of the largest auto parts companies in the country should be. He should have realized from that fact alone what he was walking into.

If who she was hadn't been enough of a clue for him, in addition to the company she owned, he should have guessed just from the car she was sporting around in like it was nothing. New, and he had no doubt she'd bought it new, that little sports car of hers probably cost more than he earned in two years working the circuit, maybe three.

It didn't matter if he was in line to inherit one third of his grandfather's twenty-five thousand acre ranch, he knew this place, in this location, was worth far more than his spread would ever be.

Yet CeCe Cole, in spite of all her lavish things, was still the most discontented woman he'd ever come across, thereby proving money didn't buy happiness.

He tried to keep that surreal knowledge in mind as he rolled down his window. "Where should I park?"

She'd pulled her car into a bay in a stone building that matched the house, but on a smaller scale.

Closing the automatic door with the push of a button, she walked to his truck, teetering in her heels on the cobblestones. The drive was pretty, but she'd be lucky if she didn't break an ankle trying to get from the car to the house.

"In front of the carriage house is fine."

A carriage house. So that's what high falutin' folks called their fancy garages.

She continued, "Pull it up close though. The landscapers should be here one day this week and they'll need room to get past."

"The landscapers. Got it." Shaking his head at that new piece of information, Wade pulled up to where she'd said.

CeCe was breaking Wade of all sorts of firsts that, at forty years old, he'd never expected. First sex in an elevator. First time he'd said yes to willingly sticking around for more than a night during what he'd intended to be a one-night stand. And, apparently, his first lay who was as rich as King Midas and all his gold.

All in the span of twenty-four hours. It was turning out to be one hell of a week and it was only Monday.

He locked the doors and pocketed the key to his pick-up. Why he did that, he didn't know. It wasn't as if anyone was going to steal his truck in this neighborhood.

Wade sauntered toward the front door of a building that

looked more like a museum than a home.

No wonder she felt lonely here. The size alone would isolate a person even if it was full of people. But it was also no surprise she'd chosen for them to spend the week here instead of over at his crappy hotel room.

Hell, he'd been happy it had a coffee maker and that the room was clean. Both of those amenities put the hotel steps above some of the places he'd stayed.

Obviously, CeCe had a far different level of comparison when it came to accommodations.

Truth be told, it was a little mind boggling, but none of this shit mattered to him. If where they stayed had a bed, he was happy. A bed with a hellcat like CeCe in it with him, even better.

His duffle bag in one hand, Wade reached where she was opening the front door. "Nice place you got here."

She snorted. "Wanna buy it? It's on the market. Good price too. Divorce sale."

He heard the bitterness in her tone and realized this house was probably nothing more than one big bad memory to her. A constant reminder of her pain, like a splinter trapped beneath her skin.

Wade could fix that—or at least ease the pain a bit. He'd be more than happy to supply her with new memories to replace the old.

He glanced around, as if considering the place. "Hmm, interesting. Let me talk to my investment manager and see what he says. I'll uh, have my people call your people."

She rolled her eyes at him before taking a step inside. Smiling, he followed her in and pushed the door closed behind him before dropping his bag on the floor. "Where first?"

She watched him with widened eyes as he backed her up against the wall. "Excuse me?"

He positioned one thigh between her legs—which was becoming his favorite place to be. He had her pinned in place by his body, bracketed between the arms he braced against the wall.

Wade leaned low and ran his mouth over her throat before saying, "Which room do you want to christen first? Of course, it doesn't matter which is first I guess. We're going to get to all of them eventually. At least, we will if I have anything to say about it. That okay with you?"

He latched onto her neck with his teeth.

She drew in a stuttering breath. "How about the bedroom?"

Enjoying how easy it was to get this woman revved up, he smiled. "Oh, we'll get there eventually. But I'm in the mood to explore other venues a bit first."

He glanced around him at the cold marble foyer, so empty sounds echoed within it. With its single table in the center, decorated with a glass vase filled with fresh flowers, Wade decided this room didn't hold much appeal for what he had in mind.

Time to go exploring. Or, he had an even better idea. Given the size of this place, it might be better if he enlisted CeCe's help. "Your ex-husband have a home office here?"

"Yes. He liked to hide in there for hours. Probably watching gay porn on his computer."

Wade frowned. "When you said he'd cheated on you, I'd assumed it was with a woman."

"Oh, it was. Many women. That doesn't mean anything."

Wade let that comment go as the ramblings of a bitter divorcee, though he had to admit he'd most likely look at John Cole and wonder a little bit the next time he saw him in the chute seats at an event. "Anyway, show me this office."

"Why?" she asked.

"His desk still in there?"

"Yes."

"Then I'm going to fuck you on top of it. That okay?" he asked.

Her eyes widened just a bit before she took a step forward. "This way."

Grinning, Wade grabbed his bag—because that's where

the condoms were—and followed. He had a feeling he was going to thoroughly enjoy his room-by-room tour of the house. So would CeCe.

CHAPTER ELEVEN

The revenge sex in the office didn't take all that long.

Wade had been more interested in the conceptual satisfaction than the actual physical gratification.

He got plenty of both by taking her on her cheating ex-husband's desk and, as it turned out, also in his desk chair while CeCe straddled him.

What he lacked in finesse he made up for in enthusiasm to make sure she wouldn't forget the day anytime soon.

Kinky office sex was yet another first for him, but there was something to be said for a nice big bed. That was the main reason he suggested that they adjourn to the bedroom the minute he was done claiming John Cole's former office in the name of CeCe—or maybe in the name of Wade Long. He liked that last idea.

CeCe didn't argue with his plan to head to the bedroom. Probably because chair sex and desk sex hadn't yielded any orgasms for her.

In his defense he had been working with a handicap. He could sense that she hated the office as much as she hated her ex-husband. He could see that in the set of her jaw and the flashing of her eyes.

Inside her bedroom, which was about as big as he expected it to be in such a grand house, she seemed more relaxed. Calmer. And a little aggressive, which Wade was fine with once in a while.

She stared at him now through eyes so narrowed she looked even more like a predator than her usual hellcat. "Take off your clothes."

He was surprised at her order, but never opposed to being naked in the presence of a beautiful woman. "Okay."

After dropping his bag on the floor and tossing the box of condoms on the nightstand, Wade proceeded to strip for her. He didn't miss how her gaze followed every move. He also didn't miss how she was still dressed.

"*Quid pro quo*, beautiful."

CeCe cocked one perfectly shaped brow high. "Fancy words for a bullfighter."

She had basically just insulted him. He'd deal with that and her once they were both naked.

"Yup. They mean you'd better get your clothes off too." He stopped in the middle of unzipping his jeans and waited.

Finally, CeCe reached for the zipper on her skirt.

"Good girl." He grinned and finished stripping, anxious to see if the big bed felt as soft as it looked.

Reclining on his back, he sunk into a mass of pillows and goose down. It sure beat the hell out of the hotel bed and bedding.

CeCe followed him onto the mattress, stalking toward him with the look of a cat on the prowl. She stopped mid-way up his body and he grinned when he realized her intent.

He'd enjoy being buried between those pretty lips of hers. That was one thing they hadn't gotten to last night or this morning.

As she lowered her lips over his cock, he squeezed his eyes shut to better concentrate on the sensations.

On the skill of the woman sucking him off as she stroked up and down with both hand and mouth.

On the feel of the wet heat surrounding him.

On the finger CeCe was slowly sneaking back behind his balls before she tried poking it inside a place he didn't want it to go.

"Uh, where you think you're going down there?" He reached down and grasped her wrist, pulling her hand a safe distance away.

She lifted her head and slipped her mouth off his cock. "You'll see."

"Oh no, I won't."

"Trust me. You'll like it." She smiled as she went right back to what she'd been doing before he had stopped her—poking at his hole with one finger of her right hand.

With her left hand, she reached for the table next to the bed. When she pulled open the drawer, he glanced inside and saw an eye-opening array of objects of the sexual nature.

Some things he could identify immediately. Others were too baffling to even guess at. None of it was anything he intended to experience by being on the receiving end. If that was CeCe's intention, she was going to be disappointed.

Now him using them on CeCe would be another story.

When she reached for the bottle of lube in the drawer, he knew it was time to put an end to her attempts.

He wouldn't like what she was playing at, but he knew something he would like. Very much. Something he didn't get to do nearly enough.

"If that's the area you're interested in, I surely can oblige." He sat up and maneuvered so CeCe was on her stomach and beneath him in seconds.

It hadn't even been hard to accomplish.

Wade had grown up with an older brother and he had also been on the wrestling team back in high school. Given that, he could switch up positions pretty good against an equally matched opponent.

Getting one underweight, off-guard woman facedown beneath him presented no challenge whatsoever.

Before she knew what was happening, he'd shoved a pillow under her hips and had the creamy flesh of her ass cheeks spread wide. "Mmm. Oh, yeah. Look at that tight little hole just waiting for me."

"Wade." She tried to flip over beneath him, but he was sitting on her legs.

Reaching for the drawer, he grabbed the bottle of lube she had been aiming for just moments before with the intent of using it on him.

"Wade, I don't like this." She sounded breathless as she gripped the sheets in tight fists.

What was good for the goose was good for the gander.

"That's funny since you assured me that I'd like it while you were trying to do it to me." He flipped the top open and wet his finger with a small amount of the slippery liquid.

Circling her puckering hole, he got her nice and lubed up before pushing just the tip of his finger inside. He pushed his finger deeper, past the first knuckle, as his cock grew impossibly harder.

He twisted his finger as he fucked her real slowly with it. He pulled out, and then pushed back in, slow and easy, gentling her into accepting his finger in preparation for something much bigger. "This feel good?"

"No." Her breath caught in her throat and Wade couldn't help feeling satisfied.

Smiling, he shook his head at her answer. "Liar."

Wade knew the difference between the sounds of pain and pleasure. He added a second finger, enjoying how he could coax her body into accepting him. How she went from being so tight he could barely get a fingertip in, to now when he was able to push three fingers inside her.

Pulling his fingers out of her, he leaned back. He made short work of donning a condom before he grabbed the bottle and drizzled on a generous amount of lube.

Soon he was back, positioning his tip against her tight hole. She went still. For a few seconds, he wasn't even sure she was breathing. "Wade, please."

For the first time since knowing her, Wade heard uncertainty in her voice.

"What's wrong, beautiful?" He didn't lesson the pressure of his cock against her tight hole, but he did smooth his other hand down her spine. Leaning low, he ran his mouth over the smooth skin of her shoulder.

"I've never—"

"Then how do you know you won't like it?" He tongued her earlobe while enjoying the feel of sliding his cock against her crevice. Not entering her just yet.

"I'm scared." It might be the most genuinely true thing she'd ever said to him.

"Nothing to be scared about, I promise. We'll take it real slow." He brushed a kiss against her ear and then decided to lighten the mood with a joke. "Besides, I heard it only hurts in the beginning but it's worth it in the end."

Of course every joke had a little truth in it and from what he'd been told by the women he'd done this with, what he'd just said was true.

Better get this started before she bolted, which was a real possibility. Leaning back, he used both hands to spread her flesh wide. That gave him one hell of a view when he pushed forward.

She drew in a sharp breath. "Wade—"

He stopped and held, waiting for her body to get used to the feel of him inside her. "Just breathe."

He was surprised when she did as he asked. He felt her draw in a deep breath. He took advantage of it by sliding in farther.

She rocked forward to pull away. He held on to those beautiful hips of hers and kept her right where he needed her to be.

While reaching for the lube, he got a glimpse of the contents of her nightstand one more time. There was some scary looking shit in there.

Remembering she'd been about to stick at least her fingers and possibly any number of those things from her drawer inside him, he figured the woman had better be willing to take it herself.

He drizzled a stream of cool lubricant over where they were joined and then drove in the rest of the way as CeCe dragged in a breath. He held there, wanting nothing more than to absorb the feeling of how nice and tight she was and how damn good it felt to be inside her.

Thrusting would feel even better, for him anyway. He had a suspicion she wasn't ready for that quite yet.

Wade ran his palms over her ass and settled them on the swell of her hips. The beauty of the sight in front of him made it hard to hold still.

"The hard part's done, beautiful. It'll start feeling better now."

"I don't believe you." Even with him buried balls deep in her ass and with her face down on the pillow he heard the attitude in her voice.

How he loved a woman with attitude, especially in this particular position.

"Then I guess I'll have to prove it to you."

Her breathing was fast, but he knew it wasn't all from pleasure. Not yet anyway. She was still scared. But it would be good for her soon, if he had any say in the matter.

Remaining fully seated inside her, Wade reached around with one hand.

Intent on making her come so she could enjoy this as much as he intended to, he slipped a finger between her lips and found her clit.

She let out a small groan the moment he made contact.

"Feel good?"

"No."

He shook his head as he heard the lie.

Her breath quickened with every stroke of his finger on her clit, each tiny gasp tinged with a small sound that had him wanting to fuck her.

"The vibrator."

He barely heard her. "What do you want, darlin'?"

She angled her head and reached one hand toward the nightstand. "Hand me a vibrator from in the drawer."

Her request surprised him, but hell, he wasn't about to argue.

There were more than a few items to choose from. "Which one?"

"The bullet."

Personally, he wasn't all that familiar with sex toys, but what she'd asked for was pretty self-explanatory.

Glancing in the drawer, he saw there was only one item that looked anything like a bullet to him. Luckily he'd grown up around hunting rifles, so bullets were something with which he was familiar. He grabbed it and handed it to her.

Wade had to admit that she knew her toys. Without looking she somehow turned on the vibe, even though he hadn't noticed any on/off switch himself.

He heard the sound as it fired to life. He sure as hell felt it as she pressed it against her clit. It vibrated all the way through her body and into his cock buried deep inside her.

She reacted to the stimulation almost immediately. It was as if she relaxed and tensed at the same time.

He gave her a minute before he couldn't stand the wait anymore. Then he began to move inside her, slow because she was tight and because it felt too amazing to risk coming too soon.

Her muscles clenched around him. He felt the first waves of the orgasm ripple through her, squeezing him in a rhythm that matched his strokes inside her.

She cried out, loud and deep. The sound alone was enough to send a tingle through him. That combined with her body milking him brought everything to an end too quickly.

His voice soon joined hers as he came right along with her.

Even more amazing was how she continued to pulsate around him. She came until she finally pulled the bullet away.

Damn, he needed to invest in some toys if this was the result.

She dropped the vibe amid the bedding where it continued to buzz until she finally got it turned off.

He was panting as he collapsed over her back. His faded erection, still nestled inside her, slipped out.

Even with as spent as he was from that incredible encounter he still managed, "Told you you'd like it."

Breathless beneath him she turned her head enough to say, loud and clear, "Fuck you."

He laughed. "Is that an invitation? Because if it is, I'm gonna need a minute to recover."

She flipped over, her eyes flashing with anger. "I told you I didn't want to do that and you did it anyway."

Wade's laughter died quickly. Accusations like this were serious. They'd ruined better men than him.

"No, CeCe. Not once did you ask me to stop in so many words. If you had, I would have."

Yes, she'd said she'd never done it. And yes, she'd told him she was scared. She told him when it hurt, which he'd warned her it would, but then she'd told him to get her the vibrator.

Never had the word *stop* or anything equivalent come out of her mouth. If it had, he would have be perfectly happy to abandon exploring new territory with her and proceed the old fashioned way.

She refused to answer him, breaking eye contact to stare into the corner of the room.

"CeCe." He held her chin and forced her to look at him. "Did you tell me to stop?"

She pressed her lips together and finally said, "No."

"And did I lie to you? Didn't it stop hurting just like I said it would?"

Drawing in a breath that had her nostrils flaring, she gritted out between clenched teeth, "Yes."

"And did you come?" He knew the answer to that. There had been no missing it, but he wanted her to say it out loud.

"Yes." This answer contained even more venom than the last.

She was pissed and he knew why. CeCe Cole was the kind of woman who was used to getting her way. She'd never take kindly to having someone say no to her and he had during her exploratory probing of his ass.

Then he'd gone one better and given her a taste of her own medicine.

It was unfortunate for CeCe that she and Wade were the same when it came to wanting to be in control. That was one reason why he could appreciate so well exactly how she was feeling right now.

He pulled off the used condom with a snap and tossed it into the garbage pail on the other side of the nightstand. "I'm sorry you were scared and I'm very sorry it hurt you."

She pulled her mouth to one side, as if she didn't believe him.

That was a shame. He'd said it, and meant it, but that was all he could do. He wasn't into groveling. Especially not at the feet of a spoiled brat of a woman.

He'd have to make it up to her in another way. Reaching down, he grabbed each of her ankles in one hand and yanked her legs apart.

Her eyes flew wide. "What are you doing?"

Leaning low, he looked up at her from between her spread thighs. "I think that's pretty obvious."

A crease formed between her brows. "Are you crazy? I'm mad at you."

"I'm aware." He smiled before he opened her wide with his thumbs and drew her clit between his lips.

She could be as pissed off as she wanted, but he could still make her body sing.

Wade proved the truth of that now as she went from raring for a fight, to sighing in pleasure in under a minute.

He felt the fight leave her as CeCe tipped up her hips, just enough to press against his mouth. He was glad she couldn't see his smile over her surrender to him.

Gloating over winning this round would probably earn him a smack up side the head, if not worse.

The vixen could throw him out of her house if she wanted to.

That would be a shame, since he had every intention of sinking into this woman as often as possible before he had to leave for the next event.

He'd never admit it to her, but even with as amazing as this last round had been, one time would never be enough for him to get his fill of her.

CeCe's breathing quickened and in a few minutes she was gasping. He felt her tense and knew she was close.

"Stop." With one shove of a hand, she pushed his head away.

"Nope. Not until you come." He was about to go back to work when she tangled her fingers in his hair and tugged.

"Fuck me."

If her pulling his hair hadn't gotten his attention, that request would have. Raising his eyes to look at her, he saw the need in her heavily lidded gaze. "Gladly."

She drew her brows low. "The regular way. Not that other way."

He smiled as he worked his way up her body, grabbing a condom along the way. "Yeah, I figured that."

"And don't look so pleased with yourself. I'm still mad at you." She grit out the words from between tight lips.

The smile he couldn't control grew wider as he rolled on the condom. He always had liked the tough challenges. "You still don't get it, do you?"

"Get what?" Her scowl deepened.

"The more you hate me, the more you bitch and act like a hellcat, the harder it gets me." He watched as her gaze dropped to the evidence of his words bobbing between them. A nearly feral groan rumbled from deep within him. "God, I'm gonna fuck you so hard."

She looked as if she was about to lay into him some more but CeCe never got the chance to holler. He covered her mouth with his and slid home, rough and fast, driving the breath from her lungs.

One of her fists hit his arm, before she sank into his kiss. His tongue tangled with hers, plunging into her mouth.

She met the stroke of his cock thrust for thrust and a realization hit him. He might never grow tired of fucking this woman.

Of course, if he spent too much time with her out of bed there was a good chance he'd end up wanting to kill her and her him.

But in bed they were damn good together. Two fucked up people fucking. A perfect match.

CHAPTER TWELVE

CeCe woke to an empty bed and a feeling of disappointment. Wade wasn't there. He'd probably left. She shouldn't have expected him to stay. He wasn't the type.

She was a stupid woman to assume—

Her self-loathing was interrupted when she drew in her first deep breath of the morning and was hit with the aroma of fresh brewed coffee and something else. Bacon?

Glancing at the clock on the nightstand she saw it was early. Her housekeeper wouldn't be here yet. Maria would make coffee whenever she arrived, but she knew better than to cook bacon. CeCe wouldn't eat that. It was only in the house because Maria sometimes made spinach salad and crumbled it on top.

Wade enjoyed some meat with his breakfast though. She'd learned that yesterday when he'd taken her to the diner and forced her to eat for breakfast more than she usually did in an entire day.

Could that be Wade in the kitchen? Cooking?

She swung her legs over the edge of the mattress and felt the pull of sore muscles. Sex with the man was proving to be a pretty vigorous full body workout.

Padding naked across the room, she grabbed a robe from the hook by the door and slipped it on. She was too curious to take the time to dress.

The floors were cool against her bare feet as she made her way down the stairs and across the foyer to the kitchen.

He glanced up when she entered the room. "Good morning, beautiful. How's your ass feel today?"

Even with how hot he looked manning a frying pan, shirtless, his question had her frowning. "I'm still mad at you about that. And do you have to be so crude all the time?"

"My apologies." Wade cleared his throat and performed a sweeping bow. "How is your delicate rectal region this fine morning, my lady?"

She wrinkled her nose. "Ew. That's worse. And it's sore, thank you very much."

He stepped forward and reached out to draw her to him. Wade kissed her hard while holding her forearms with both his hands. After he broke the kiss, he leaned his forehead against hers in an act that had her confused. Wade could be a sex driven pig one moment, and incredibly sweet the next.

"I'm sorry, darlin'."

She pulled her mouth to the side. "Are you?"

"Yeah, I am." He grinned, negating the sincerity she'd heard in his words before. "While you're sore we can't do it again."

And the pig was back.

She scowled. "Oh, we are never doing that again."

He bobbed his head to one side. "Eh. We'll see. You ready for bacon?"

Dropping his hold on her, Wade spun back to the counter.

"I don't usually eat bacon."

His gaze dropped down her body. "Yeah, I guessed that, judging by the look of you."

"Stop saying that."

"Saying what? That you don't eat enough? No can do, beautiful. You need to eat so you have energy because while I'm around, you're gonna need it."

That raised a very good question. "And how long will you be around?"

Wade flipped off the burner and turned, leaning back against the edge of the counter. "If I've overstayed my welcome, just say the word and I'm gone."

The serious tone and steady stare he leveled on her told CeCe he thought she wanted him to leave. As annoying as he was, that wasn't what she'd meant.

"I didn't say that. I was just wondering."

Wade watched her for a few seconds before nodding. "A'ight but I meant what I said. Just tell me to go and I'm gone. I have a day or two before I'll have to leave in order to drive to the next venue in time."

Now that he said it, she was pretty sure she knew he had an event Friday he needed to drive to, but she'd forgotten.

In her defense, it was very distracting trying to hold a conversation in the kitchen with a man dressed in nothing but briefs.

Perhaps if his muscles weren't so big and hard it might be easier. And if the bruise on his ribs didn't remind her every time she saw it just how crazy it was when he threw his body in front of a charging bull to save a rider's life. Crazy, but kind of hot.

Darn it. Now she wanted him again.

As he smiled and moved toward her, she had a feeling she might get exactly what she wanted. He lifted her up and set her on the counter just to the side of all his breakfast preparations.

Stepping in between her thighs, Wade moved in for a kiss. At the same time, he ran his hand up the inside of her thigh.

"What about the bacon?" she asked, not really caring.

"It'll hold. I'm hungry for something else." He moved to nibbling on her neck while slipping his other hand inside her robe to fondle her breast. "Mmm, I like this easy access attire."

Leaning back, he untied the belt and pushed the sides of her robe open to feast on her breasts. One tug on her nipple with his mouth and she was a goner. She exhaled on a moan.

She felt him smile against her breast. The man truly enjoyed making her lose control. She should probably be grateful for that. It meant he tried to do it often. Her pleasure had never really been John's concern.

The sound of a gasp from the doorway brought CeCe's head around.

Her housekeeper stood wide-eyed in the doorway. "Mrs. Cole."

CeCe pushed Wade back and yanked the sides of her robe together, tying the belt tight. "Maria."

Shit. CeCe had lost track of the time. Wade was quite the distraction.

It was Tuesday and Maria worked Tuesday through Saturday, but CeCe didn't realize it was late enough for her to be here already.

"What time is it? Are you early?"

"No, ma'am. It's almost eight. You say I must be here by eight to make your coffee before you leave for work."

She couldn't fault her employee. Those were Maria's instructions, but today, work was the dead last thing on CeCe's mind.

She got a glimpse of Wade's amused expression as he remained right where he had been, between her legs, preventing her from getting down off the counter.

He didn't seem at all disturbed that he was standing in the kitchen wearing nothing but underwear and sporting a hard-on that Maria would have to be blind to miss.

Meanwhile, Maria looked at a complete loss at what to do and where to look as she diverted her gaze to the ceiling and then the floor.

CeCe had to get herself together. It was bad enough she hadn't gone into the office yesterday, and today wasn't looking promising for work either. The least she could do was maintain control in her own household with her staff.

"Coffee and breakfast are already made so why don't you go do whatever else you were going to do today?"

"I wash the sheets on Tuesdays."

"Good. Go do that." CeCe jumped on the task that would put her at the other end of the house.

Wade let out a soft laugh. "Good idea."

He was no doubt thinking the same thing she was. How sweaty and—God help her—full of spilled lube those bed sheets would be. After yesterday, they needed washing.

"Yes, ma'am." With one more quick glance at Wade and CeCe, sitting on the counter where she'd never ever sat before, Maria spun and left the room.

"Oh my God." CeCe let out a deep breath. He grinned, making her mad enough to slap his arm. "It's not funny."

"It's very funny. A few minutes later and she would have gotten even more of an eyeful because I was fixin' to get creative with the maple syrup. And now that I think about it, that there bacon grease has all sorts of potential."

"Wade!"

"CeCe!" He mocked her before turning serious. "Your divorce is final. Right?"

"Yes. Of course."

"Then as a single adult you're allowed to live a little."

"Still—"

"Let it go. Don't make me distract you." His tone held a warning.

She could only imagine what distraction he'd come up with this time. If she didn't do as he asked she could find herself tied spread eagle to the table and covered in syrup.

If not being violated again by Wade with the help of bacon grease. She glared at him until, shaking his head, he moved in between her legs again.

"CeCe, you heard Maria. She's going to be busy cleaning our sex sheets. I can, and I will, take you right here, right now. Don't think I won't. So get rid of that attitude."

She didn't doubt it. Wade always seemed to get his way, no matter what she wanted. Or thought she wanted.

John had been a pussy when it came to the bedroom. She didn't quite know what to do with a man with a dominant personality—except give in.

And enjoy it. Though she'd never admit that to Wade.

He waited patiently, watching her for her answer as to whether she was going to relax and enjoy their meal or if he'd have to force her to have sex in the kitchen while Maria was just down the hall.

Quite honestly, his threat excited her. Just as much as her picturing how creative Wade might get with the various items in the kitchen at his disposal.

Damn man. He'd perverted her without her giving him permission to do so . . . and had made her come harder than she ever had in her life yesterday.

Scowling, CeCe sighed. "Okay. Fine. I'll stop worrying. Just keep that bacon grease away from me."

Wade lifted a brow. "Just hearing that come out of your pretty little mouth is giving me ideas so I really can't make any promises."

CeCe sighed deep even as her ass clenched at the thought of him sliding inside her again. "You're incredibly trying. You know that?"

"Right back at ya, beautiful." He grinned and then took a step back. Reaching for a frying pan, he glanced in her direction. "Now, how do you like your eggs?"

CHAPTER THIRTEEN

Wade stood at the window and watched the landscapers work below. The buzz and whir of their machines had started not long after the sun had risen.

CeCe moved up beside him. "What's so interesting out there?"

She rested her hand on his back, lightly, barely touching him, but he was hyper aware of its presence, and hers.

"Your work crew. Do you realize you have as many men working here as my granddaddy has working his cattle ranch?"

By Wade's estimate, CeCe employed about one man per acre. Of course, at the ranch, the grass was meant to feed the cattle, not to look pretty. And hers certainly did look pretty.

Dark green and lush in spite of the drought and neat as a pin. There'd be not one blade out of place after these men got done.

"You never told me your family has a ranch."

"You never asked." He turned and wrapped his arms around her, pulling her close. "Does Maria work today?"

"Yes."

"Then I guess it'll have to be here then."

"What will have to be in here?"

"Our morning exercise." He could see by her expression she knew exactly what kind of exercise he was referring to.

"Still insatiable, I see."

"Yup. That's the meaning of the word insatiable, beautiful. Never able to be satisfied. So why do you keep acting surprised that I haven't changed?"

Today was Thursday, and he'd only been with CeCe since Sunday night. Not nearly long enough to have his fill of her yet.

Of course, there had been a few women in his sordid past he'd had quite enough of after an hour, so perhaps he shouldn't be so presumptuous.

"Because you continue to surprise me, Wade Long."

"Right back at ya, sister." He grinned while backing her toward the bed. "Now hush up and let me love you before I have to leave."

"Leave?" Her brow creased.

He hadn't mentioned it before because he had a feeling it was going to put a damper on things. He was sorry he'd mentioned it now, before the sex.

A man of his vast experience with women should have known better. Always bring up the tough subjects after sex, not before.

"Event starts tomorrow night. It's an eleven-hour drive. I need to get going today."

"Of course." She nodded but somehow he didn't believe that was the end of this conversation.

He trailed a finger over her bare thigh to distract her. Him too. He wasn't looking forward to the end of this thing—whatever this thing was.

A fling. A relationship. Something in between.

Whatever it was, it ended when he left.

Yeah, he might run across her again next time he was in California. And if she were still single maybe they'd spend another night or two in bed.

Two things made that unlikely. A woman like CeCe

wouldn't be single for long. She was rich, attractive and needy. Any number of men would line up to fulfill all of her needs.

More, she didn't seem like the casual, booty call type. He couldn't show up a couple of times a year. What would he say to her? *Hey, I'm in town for the weekend. Wanna fuck?*

Yeah, she'd lay into him for that, he was sure. Maybe that wouldn't be that bad. Just thinking about the daggers she'd shoot him with those eyes that showed every emotion so clearly had him getting hard.

Moving his hand up beneath the hem of her sexy lace nightie, Wade didn't stop until he reached the heat of her core.

At his first contact with her clit, CeCe hissed in a sharp breath.

How he loved the way she reacted to his every touch. How her eyes lost focus and her lips parted as she gasped for breath.

Wade brushed kisses along her neck and was treated with her soft moan. "Do you realize how fucking beautiful you look when you come?"

"Not coming yet," she gasped.

He smiled at how, even now, she had to be contrary. "You will be soon."

"We'll see." She drew in a shaky breath as a crease formed between her brows.

He recognized that particular frown. He'd seen it enough the past few days. She was close. All she'd need was a little push to send her over the edge.

Wade leaned in and scraped his teeth over the skin of her throat. She tipped her hips up and started to shake and he knew he'd won this round.

Though, there were certainly no losers in this particular sport.

CeCe was still gasping when Wade took her mouth in a hard kiss. He hadn't ever been with a woman he enjoyed kissing as much as he liked fucking.

Damned if he knew why, but CeCe's mouth called to him. Made him want to possess her lips as much as he wanted to sink his cock into her.

It was the strangest thing but he didn't fight the urge. Instead, he tossed her on the bed and settled his body over her.

Tangling his fingers in her hair, he thrust his tongue against hers. He'd eventually have to get a condom because he had every intention of being inside this woman at least one more time before he left her. But for now, this was good. Really good.

His intention was to take his time, but it didn't work out that way. He found himself unable to wait. He needed to have her. All of her. Not soon, not later, but now.

That's when he knew he was in trouble.

It was going to be harder to leave this woman than he'd ever anticipated. He was almost saddened at the thought of leaving.

When had the end of a one-night, or even a four-night stand ever affected him like this?

Never.

And that was exactly why he had to leave.

Between both of their track records of failed marriages and the differences between him and CeCe, they were doomed.

If they ever got off the ground at all.

Kick ass sex, their being incredible in bed together—and out of it—wasn't good enough for the long term.

They might be okay for a little while, but in the long run it would all go to shit just like every other relationship he'd ever tried and failed at.

Wade's thoughts had put a damper on what was most likely his last time with CeCe, but he hadn't been able to control the rambling in his head.

Taking back control of his wayward mind, he focused on CeCe, on every detail about her. Memorizing the things he'd relive later when he was behind the wheel for that long ass drive.

How damn long her legs were. The longest legs he'd ever seen on a woman and he'd seen quite a few.

How fair her skin was. So pale she'd burn to a crisp if she ever spent time working outdoors under the sun on the ranch. Not that she was likely to ever do that, which brought Wade full circle to how impossibly different they were.

When he left and she finally got back to her life and her job, she'd be up in her fancy corporate offices and he'd be rolling around down in the dirt. Literally.

She opened her eyes. The big blue orbs focused on him. "You okay?"

"Sure. Why you ask?"

"I don't know. You're not as—enthusiastic as usual. I thought maybe your ribs hurt." She ran a finger over the bruises that were beginning to turn all sorts of pretty colors, just like they always did. "It looks painful."

"That little old bruise? Nah. I'm used to being banged up. And I got to be wreck of the night so, you know, that made it all worth it." As she rolled her eyes at him, Wade forced a smile and lied, "Don't you worry about me. I've never felt better. Let me show you."

He reached for a condom and decided to try to turn that lie into reality.

Wade planted his palms on skin so soft it felt like silk, but with the added benefit of a heat that fabric didn't possess.

The warmth of her skin was only surpassed by the heat that surrounded him as he pushed inside her.

His lids drifted closed from the sensation, but the sound of her soft gasp as he entered her had him forcing his eyes open again. CeCe was beautiful at anytime, but even more so while he loved her.

As much as he'd tried to take his time, it was impossible. He lost his control and pounded himself to conclusion much too soon, which is what always seemed to happen with CeCe.

The orgasm rocked him to the core. Not just his body, but somehow the rest of him too.

He didn't know if it was his head or his heart—maybe it was his very soul—but some part of him was trying to grasp onto CeCe and never let her go. Skip the event, move in here and never leave.

That irrational thought prompted Wade to roll off her before he lost all common sense. "I'm gonna shower."

Still gasping from the loving, CeCe nodded.

Before the need to shower was the need for something to drink. Alcohol might have helped more, but instead he pulled on shorts and made his way to the kitchen for a bottle of water from the fridge. He'd worked up a thirst.

Barely through the doorway of the kitchen, Wade realized it was a good thing he'd taken the time to put on shorts. A shirt might have been good too. "Mornin', Maria."

"Good morning, Mr. Wade. The coffee is ready."

"Thanks." He smiled. Over the past few days he'd gotten her to call him Wade, but dropping the mister seemed beyond her.

He grabbed the water and also pulled out the container of half and half for CeCe's coffee.

Scooping sugar into CeCe's mug, he had to think his bringing her coffee in bed would win him some pretty big brownie points.

Maybe enough she'd hop in the shower with him. The stall was certainly big enough for two and those multiple pulsating heads held all sorts of potential.

With CeCe's coffee prepared just the way she liked it, he picked up her mug and his water bottle and turned to find Maria smiling at him.

That could be because he was once again only partially dressed in front of the poor older woman, but she should be used to it by now. She'd seen him in all sorts of states of undress over the past half a week. Today's shorts were a huge step up from the underwear he'd been wearing the day they first met.

Pausing, he raised a brow in her direction and waited.

She pressed her hands to her cheeks, shaking her head.

"I'm so sorry. It's just, I'm happy you're here, Mr. Wade."

"Well, I'm glad. But why is that?"

"Because of Mrs. Cole. She's happy since you're here."

"Is she? How can you tell?" Wade knew CeCe had been well fucked since he'd arrived but he didn't think Maria was the kind of person who would bring that up.

"She smiles now. She never used to before. Not really. Not all the way to her heart." Maria tapped her own chest with a fist.

The comment brought a lump to Wade's throat. "Um, I'm gonna bring her this before it gets cold."

Blowing out a breath, he headed down the hallway. Shower, pack and then he had to leave. If he didn't do it now, he had a bad feeling he wouldn't be able to.

CHAPTER FOURTEEN

"How have you been feeling?" Dr. Stein asked.

"Fine." CeCe pedaled faster on the exercise bike as the therapist eyed her more closely.

"Are you sure?" The older man, who looked too much like Freud to not be a good therapist, lifted one bushy brow.

"Yes. I'm fine. Why do you ask?"

"If you pedal any faster you might lift off."

"I missed my workout four days this week. I have to make up for the days I took off."

"And why did you miss your workout?"

Talking was difficult while pedaling at this speed, but the Dr. Stein had agreed to not only meet at her home, but also during her work out.

This was multi-tasking in the extreme, but it had been her idea, so CeCe had no choice but to talk.

The Cole name definitely had its benefits. And its downside.

One of those negatives was her packed schedule as she tried to handle all the things she'd ignored while playing bed sports with Wade.

Dr. Stein had asked her a question, and she had no choice

but to answer. Therapy only worked when she was totally honest—with the doctor and with herself.

CeCe threw caution to the wind and let the truth fly. "I spent the first half of the week in bed with a totally inappropriate man."

She watched for a reaction, but the damn man had the best poker face of anyone she'd ever seen.

"And what made this man inappropriate, in your opinion?"

She'd dropped a verbal bomb and that was what he honed in on? Fine. If he was really interested, CeCe had a whole list.

"Well, he was a complete stranger. I met him, followed him to a bar, let him buy me shots and then had sex with him in his truck in the parking lot, all within the span of about six hours."

At this point, it had become a goal to shock this man. That confessional should have done it. Unfortunately, it didn't seem to.

The doctor nodded calmly and asked, "What else?"

"Well . . ." She seemed to have run out of things. Grasping for anything, she said, "He's a bullfighter."

His brow drew down. "In Mexico?"

She couldn't help but smile. "No. That's what they call the guys in the rodeo who distract the bull and protect the riders."

"Ah." He nodded. "And that occupation made him inappropriate for you?"

"No, I guess not." She slowed the speed with which she was pedaling. She was finding it hard to think. When she thought about it, Wade himself wasn't the problem.

He was age appropriate. He had a decent job. She'd lost count of how many times he'd given her compliments—not the disingenuous ones so many men gave, but compliments that rang sincere.

Of course many of them had been during sex.

Wade cooked and worried that she didn't eat enough. He even took notice of exactly how she took her coffee and managed to get it right—something even her assistant at work hadn't managed.

Yesterday morning when she suggested that Maria had prepared her cup of coffee and he'd just carried it in, he'd made a point of correcting her.

She'd even asked Maria later that day and the maid had confirmed Wade had prepared it himself with no coaching on her part.

"What are you thinking, CeCe?" the doctor prompted.

"That maybe the problem isn't the men I've chosen since my divorce, but me."

He nodded, looking pleased with her confession. "And what problem do you see in yourself?"

"I'm too eager to jump in with both feet." She didn't even have to think about that answer. She knew she was too quick to jump into bed. To try to force what was just sex into the start of a relationship.

"What do you think you should do about that?"

She paid this man an awful lot for him to do nothing but ask a lot of questions and nod when what she really wanted was for him to just tell her what to do to feel better.

Even so, she answered his question. "I've already done it."

"Done what?"

"When he left yesterday, I let him go." She didn't try to convince him to stay. Didn't offer to go with him. Didn't ask him to come back after the event.

She'd just kissed him goodbye and then watched him drive away . . . then she'd curled in a ball in bed for the rest of the day.

Maybe she hadn't quite handled her issues yet after all.

CeCe realized she'd stopped pedaling completely. She'd been so deep in her own thoughts. She started again and raised her gaze to the doctor. "So? Don't you have more questions?"

"Do you?"

At times like this, she wished her therapy included a punching bag. "Yes, as a matter of fact, I do have some questions. When am I going to be able to have a nice, normal, happy relationship?"

Or had her marriage ruined her for that forever?

Was she always going to chase the guy who was too young and completely uninterested like Aaron? Or the bad boy, free spirit who'd push her to do things she'd never done and never knew she'd wanted to before leaving her like Wade?

She wouldn't even let herself remember the ill fated revenge fucks right after the divorce. A security guard one night late at the office. One of her team of lawyers. Her personal trainer.

"That's up to you."

CeCe scowled at the typical psych babble from her doctor and didn't justify it with a comment.

He continued, "Let's get back to the man from this week."

"Wade? Why?"

He nodded and wrote something down. "Yes. Wade. Why did you choose him, in particular?"

That, for once, was a very good question. She had to think about it for a moment.

Why, when there were plenty of men at that arena—riders, association executives, media, security, and countless more—had she chosen Wade?

"I don't know. He really was obnoxious. And insulting. It's like the man took nothing seriously, including me."

"Don't you think maybe that is what attracted you to him? That he didn't take you too seriously? That the name CeCe Cole didn't influence him or have him scrambling to please you?"

"Maybe." She tried to decide if that was a good thing or a bad thing. "What's that mean?"

"That you're finally showing an interest in men who aren't subservient to you. But also that you still crave attention. Wade didn't give it to you so it made you want him." He smiled, possibly for the first time ever in her presence. "I think you've made progress."

A smile? From Dr. Stein? His odd expression had her

stopping the motion of her feet once again. "That doesn't sound like progress."

The man wobbled his head in a maybe yes, maybe no gesture.

After two years of therapy, he was finally happy. And all because her wild sexual fling had been with a man who'd challenged her and didn't bow to her wishes?

She hated to admit it, but the damn doctor might be right.

John had never challenged her. Hell, she'd acted more like the man in that relationship in the bedroom. Maybe that's why he'd sought out other women.

The security guard. The lawyer. The trainer. They'd both worked for her.

Aaron had been a kid. He'd snuck out on her in the middle of the night rather than tell her he wasn't interested.

But Wade, he'd been different. He'd controlled her and she'd liked it.

And he'd left without any promise to be back, because he was in control of what happened between them, not her.

If wanting a man like that was her future, she didn't see happiness coming anytime soon.

"So, I think we've had some very good insights and made some promising advancements today." He closed his notebook and stood from where he'd been sitting on a piece of exercise equipment in lieu of a chair.

"Our session is over?"

"Yes. Unless you had something else you needed to discuss."

Yes. Like how could she ever be happy if she couldn't control the man she feared she was falling for?

And was she really falling for Wade or did she only want him because he'd left her?

Was she just desperate for someone to love who'd love her back?

CeCe shook her head. "No. I'll have my assistant call and schedule a session for next week."

"Good. See you then."

He left and she tackled the bike again, punishing the pedals and her body—which seemed to be the only thing she had control over at the moment.

It didn't work to stop her thoughts. Her mind racing faster than her feet on the pedals, CeCe finally gave up and climbed off.

Grabbing a towel, she dabbed it over her face and neck as she made her way up the stairs to the kitchen.

"Maria."

"Yes, Mrs. Cole?"

"Do we have any bacon?"

The woman's dark brows lifted. She stood motionless for a second before scrambling toward the refrigerator. "Um, yes. I think so. I'll look."

"No rush. I'm going to take a shower but I think I'd like bacon and eggs for breakfast today before I head to the office."

"Yes, ma'am." She didn't miss Maria's smile.

CHAPTER FIFTEEN

"Damn, you look like crap." Frowning, Clint stared at Wade.

He let out a laugh. "Thanks. Nice to see you too."

"What did you do all week? You go home to the ranch?"

That was a good guess on Clint's part.

When Wade did travel home to the ranch between events he came back exhausted. There was a lot of work to be done there. On top of that, Wade's being absent so much was thrown in his face enough times by his brother to exhaust him mentally.

Wade tried to make up for the work he missed by doing double during the time he was home. Even then he knew he wasn't pulling his weight. His brother agreed and let him know it.

Yup, between the guilt and the work, Wade was beat after those trips. But today's reason for his looking like crap was one Ms. CeCe Cole.

He'd left her place later than he should have yesterday. He had trouble leaving for reasons he'd rather not think about.

Once he had finally gotten on the road, he drove straight through and didn't hit the town for the next venue until the middle of the night.

He'd checked into the hotel and crashed.

Sleeping late would have been smart, but his damn body—not to mention his mind—liked to wake up at sunrise.

Since he'd gone to bed sober and there was no hangover to sleep off, he'd gotten up. It seemed more productive than lying there thinking. Remembering CeCe. Second guessing his decision to not contact her again.

Sure, if they ran into each other at an event and one thing led to another, he'd be grateful for it. But that was all. He wouldn't set them both up for failure by pursuing more between them.

The sex had been great. That he could handle. It was that the rest was pretty damn amazing too that scared the shit out of him.

Clint was still watching him, waiting for an answer as to where he'd been and why he looked so shitty. "Nah. I kicked around California for a few days then headed here."

"Did you pick up any rodeos?"

"Nope."

The moment he said it, he realized his mistake. Clint's eyes widened and a wide grin spread across his face. "You dog, you. Who was she? From the last event?"

Crap. Wade hadn't wanted to lie, but the truth was a huge tip off. Clint had easily made the leap that the reason Wade hadn't worked any rodeos or gone home to the ranch was a woman.

Wade shook his head. "A gentleman doesn't kiss and tell."

Clint cocked one brow up. "Maybe so, which leads to my next question. Since when are you a gentleman?"

"Nice. Thanks. Love you too, buddy." Wade had walked right into the razzing by not having a good excuse as to where he'd spent the days since the last event, but it didn't mean he had to stick around for it. "See you later. I gotta change."

"Yeah. I'm sure."

Wade ignored Clint and his insinuations and headed back

toward the rider dressing room.

Even though he'd gotten to the event hours early, Wade arrived to find the dressing room already occupied. He moved to the area where one of his fellow bullfighters was lacing up his sneakers.

"Hey, Shorty."

"Hey, Wade. You have a good week?"

He wasn't going to make the same mistake twice. Wade decided to keep his answer short and sweet.

"Yup." The less specific his answer, the better. He only hoped that Shorty wouldn't follow up with another question. In fact, Wade decided to ask a question of his own and take the spotlight off himself. "You?"

The other man lifted one shoulder. "Eh, just kicked around at home. Seems there's always something that needs doing. You know?"

"I hear you." Wade nodded.

This was a good conversation. Friendly and superficial. Just how Wade liked it. If more folks would just keep their conversations like this the world would be a lot simpler place.

The conversation between Wade and Shorty fell into an easy silence as Wade stripped off his boots and jeans. He folded the clothes he'd worn to drive over and put them on the bench next to his bag.

In their place, he pulled on the long loose shorts and sneakers he wore for work.

He reached into his bag one more time and his hand connected with his jersey. He stared at it and for the first time noticed how big and bright the Cole Shock Absorbers logo and name was that was emblazoned across his back and chest and down one arm.

He'd put on this shirt dozens of times already this year, but not once had it made his gut twist the way it did today.

She was going to take a little while to forget. He'd started to suspect that before he left.

Even his usual routine wasn't enough to take his mind off her. He could only hope the action in the arena would.

Running from a rank bull intent on hooking him might be Wade's one hope to quiet his mind.

As of now, when it came to CeCe, his mind was anything but at peace.

Reminder of what he'd left or not, this was his uniform. Wade had just slipped the jersey over his head when Aaron and Garret came rambling into the room in the company of Chase Reese.

"Jesus, Aaron. Relax. Will you? You're worrying over nothing." Garret dumped his bag on the bench two over from where Wade sat.

Wade wondered what was up Aaron's ass today.

"You always say I'm worrying over nothing." Aaron scowled, dumping his own bag next to Garret's.

"I think Garret's right. We're at a new venue in a different state. CeCe was probably only there last week because it was local and the Cole's invitational." Chase's words had Wade going still and listening more closely.

It had been easy to forget CeCe's mistake with Aaron when Wade had been cocooned deep inside a world that consisted of not much more than her bedroom and kitchen.

Here, the reminder was like a bucket of ice water to the face.

Aaron shook his head. "The distance won't matter to CeCe. She flew all the way from California to the event in Georgia just last month."

"That's true too. She's got that private jet. She was hoping to initiate Aaron into the mile high club. Remember?" Garret's cocky comment, and the tone with which he delivered it, had Wade clenching his teeth.

She'd made a mistake being with Aaron, in Wade's opinion, but that didn't mean she deserved any of the shit these kids were saying about her.

Chase laughed. "I don't know, Aaron. I think I would've done it. A private jet. When will you ever get that chance again?"

"I know, right? That's what I told him. I mean yeah, she

was a bunny boiler, but still . . ."

"Garret, will you please shut up with the bunny boiler comments already. I'm sorry Mustang ever told you about that crazy stalker movie." Aaron shook his head.

"Bunny boiler. Love that expression." Chase chuckled, which only made Garret grin wider, obviously pleased with himself.

Wade breathed in deep as his blood pressure soared with every comment the boys made about CeCe.

As far as Wade was concerned, these guys all needed to shut the hell up. If they knew her at all, if they knew her the way he did, they would understand.

The things she did, the way she behaved, it was all a defense mechanism put in place to protect what he'd seen to be a delicate heart. A woman desperate to love and be loved.

And what the fuck was happening to him? It was as if he'd turned into some kind of quack psychologist or something.

He needed to get out of here before he got so mad at these kids he did something foolish. That could include anything from taking a swing at them to telling them off, which would only tip off everyone as to where he'd spent the week and with whom.

His judgment was clouded. If it remained so, it would affect his performance. His job required quick thinking as much as fast feet.

If he was distracted by these kids and their brat attitudes it could mean the difference between any of them walking out of the arena versus being carried out on a stretcher.

Wade had a feeling maintaining focus on anything was going to be a challenge today.

He blew out a breath and stood. "I'm gonna head out and take a look at the bulls."

Shorty nodded. "See you out there."

CHAPTER SIXTEEN

CeCe walked past her assistant's desk. The chair was empty.

In fact, there was no one around the immediate area outside her office.

Not a surprise. CeCe hadn't been there all week. Her employees probably didn't expect her to show up to work on a Friday after taking four days off.

Her little sojourn at home with Wade had probably set the workload back days. Though, honestly, she should be able to trust them to keep the company running in her absence.

She made her way to the kitchen area and reached to take a mug down from the cabinet. There was coffee in the pot and it was steaming hot and smelled fresh so someone was in the office.

Glancing at the clock, she took note of the time. It was late enough the place should be bustling. She filled the mug and was just reaching for the handle on the door of the fridge when the sound of conversation had her turning.

A stream of people filed down the hallway from the direction of the conference room.

Maggie broke off from the crowd and rushed to her.

"Ms. Cole, I didn't know you'd be in today." She reached for the fridge, took out the cream and put it on the counter. "Let me fix your coffee and bring it to you."

"That's fine. I might as well get it since I'm here." She frowned at the group as they dispersed. "Where was everyone?"

"The monthly sales meeting."

CeCe let her eyes drift closed. "I forgot all about it."

"It's okay. I took notes for you. I was going to email them to you as soon as I cleaned them up. I knew you'd want to be updated."

CeCe stopped with her hand on the sugar bowl. This girl wasn't so bad after all. "Good thinking. Thank you. I appreciate that."

Looking shy at the compliment, Maggie smiled. If CeCe wasn't mistaken, she actually blushed. CeCe probably didn't encourage her nearly enough.

"Thank you, ma'am. Are you sure I can't finish fixing your coffee for you and bring it to your office?"

It looked so important to her, CeCe took a step back. "Sure. That would be great. Thank you."

"You're welcome."

With nothing else to do in the kitchen, CeCe made her way back to her office.

Inside she'd barely sat when she was surprised to see that Maggie was there right behind her, bearing her coffee.

"Here you go. I hope it's the way you like it." The girl waited and watched.

CeCe figured she'd better taste it and confirm or the girl was never going to leave. She took a sip and had to admit, it was exactly as she liked it. "It's perfect. Thank you."

Again, Maggie beamed. "You're welcome. I'll go email that document to you."

CeCe nodded. "Thanks."

Looking happier than she ever had, Maggie spun and almost ran to her desk while CeCe sat and pondered what had just happened.

Wade had always been big on saying *please* and *thank you* with the waitresses the few times they'd been out to eat. Even at home with Maria.

His politeness never failed to earn him huge smiles as the women fell over themselves to try and help him more. She'd assumed it was because he was a good looking guy, but now she had to wonder if it just wasn't because he expressed his gratitude for whatever little thing they did for him, even if it was their job.

John had always expected people to do things for him, no *please* or *thank you* needed. If she looked closely at her own life, she realized she was the same way. It was hard not to expect a lot and give very little when just the mention of the Cole money had people bowing and scraping to please you.

It was a surreal world in which she lived. Yet she'd never noticed that until Wade had shown her a different perspective.

Thoughts of him had her reaching for her computer. Even as she opened a new browser there was a chant running through her head telling her not to do it. Not to search his name. Not to search where the next event was.

But even if she did find out that information, that didn't mean she was going to act upon it.

Besides, it was important to see what was happening in the sport since, technically, Cole Shocks was still a sponsor until the end of the season.

Maybe there was some useful press about the last event.

Since last weekend had been the Cole Shock Absorbers Invitational, she should really look and see what, if anything, was online about her company's participation. It might be useful to the marketing department.

With an abundance of excuses to justify her actions, CeCe opened a search window and began her investigation.

She started with a search for the bull riding association and found the official website. There was the listing of venues for the series for the remainder of the season.

The locations were all over the place. If Wade worked

every one of the events, he would have to crisscross the country and spend nearly every weekend in a different state.

Perhaps he didn't work every event.

People needed time off. Athletes especially. They needed to heal. She had no doubt he had broken ribs from the last competition. He pretended nothing was wrong but the bruises and the way he favored one side told a different story.

Why wouldn't the association force him to take time off to heal?

Maybe they didn't realize he'd been hurt. He was just the type to hide an injury from his bosses. But if he arrived there and they saw he was hurt, maybe they'd put him on leave or something.

Against her better judgment, CeCe let the nagging voice of curiosity override her common sense and she searched for his name specifically.

A search for *Wade Long* yielded a full page of results, including photos, videos, interviews with him and articles about him.

She clicked on one link with a particularly tantalizing headline. It turned out to be an article about a rider who'd been badly hurt but the reporter credited Wade with keeping the man from being injured worse or possibly killed.

CeCe's attention span for an actual newspaper lasted about as long as it took to read the headline and the lead paragraph, but she read this article from top to bottom.

She could picture Wade risking himself by diving beneath the deadly hooves of the still-bucking bull to grab the rider and pull him to safety. She'd seen him do almost as much at the last event. She still didn't understand why a man would choose that particular profession, but Wade had and evidence indicated he did it well.

The last paragraph of the article was about the charitable organization that covered the injured rider's bills while he recovered. The rider was quoted thanking Wade for saving his life and the organization for supporting him as he recovered.

There was a link for the charity. She clicked on it and, page by page, systematically devoured the information she found there.

CeCe had gotten so lost in the labyrinth of links leading to more information that the next time she broke from the search it was to see than an hour had passed and her coffee, mostly untouched, was cold. But getting more coffee was the last thing on her mind. Her thoughts were spinning with information—and with possibilities.

It was one thing to donate huge amounts of money as a sponsor that helped put on the show that the sport had become, but it was another thing to help the people who risked their lives in that sport when they needed it most.

"Maggie!" She didn't bother with the phone. She was too excited about her idea.

The girl was in her doorway within seconds. "Yes, ma'am?"

"I have an idea."

"Okay." She looked at a loss as to what to do next.

Were CeCe's ideas so few and far between that the staff didn't know how to react? She supposed they were. And actually, the last time she'd walked into the office and announced a major change it had been when she'd declared they'd no longer be sponsoring the professional bull riding association.

It was no wonder Maggie looked a bit trepidatious at CeCe's announcement.

"Schedule a meeting with finance, PR and marketing."

"Um, for when?"

"Now. Today. As soon as possible." CeCe was never one to sit on her hands once she'd decided to do something.

Maggie's eyes widened. "All right."

As the girl spun and headed back to her desk, CeCe called after her, "Thank you."

The charity website said they were always in need of donations, but CeCe had so much more in mind than simply cutting them a check. She wanted the whole shebang.

Promotional merchandise and informational booths at events. The Cole's name and logo prominently displayed everywhere, online and in person.

Personally, she wanted to use the Cole's money to help people, but the business side of her brain knew how important it was for their corporate image too.

She had a feeling the size of her donation would make it well worth the organization's while to give her anything she asked for in exchange.

CHAPTER SEVENTEEN

"Damn, Wade. What the fuck?"

At the sound of the voice behind him Wade turned and frowned at Clint. "What?"

The man shoved the door open with one shoulder. "You just let the door slam right in my face after I asked you to hold it."

Wade mumbled a cuss beneath his breath and hung his head. "Sorry. I didn't even hear you."

"Yeah, I guess not." Clint juggled the strap of the bag he held in one hand onto his shoulder. He downed the last of the energy drink he held in the other hand and then tossed the can into the garbage pail in the hallway. "Where you heading now?"

Lifting one shoulder, Wade shrugged. "I don't know. I hadn't really thought much about it."

Clint tipped his head toward the exit. "Come to the bar. That's where I'm headed."

"I don't know." Wade wobbled his head back and forth, uncertain.

"You got something better to do?" Clint asked.

Wade let out a snort. "No."

He certainly did not. All that awaited him on this Friday night was the cheap hotel room he'd checked into at midnight.

"Then come on. Shorty's meeting us there and he don't drink. That means we can get drunk and he'll drive us back to the hotel."

He couldn't argue with Clint's logic. "A'ight. Sounds good. Which place we going to?"

Clint tipped his head toward the parking lot. "Follow me over."

Wade nodded.

Hanging with the guys had to be better than sitting alone in his hotel room watching crap television and thinking about things he shouldn't.

Things always looked better from behind a glass of whisky.

Wade remembered how true that was as he tipped the glass back and felt the drink burn down his throat.

From this side of the glass filled with amber liquid, the girls on the dance floor were prettier. Shorty and Clint's jokes seemed funnier. The song the band was playing was catchier. And his forgetting a certain red head got a little easier. All after just a couple of drinks.

Of course, whisky with a beer chaser meant one thing also got more intense—his need to take a piss.

Wade pushed his chair back and stood. "I gotta take a whizz. Order another round if the waitress comes by while I'm gone."

"You got it." Clint dipped his head.

Wade steered a wide berth around the dance floor on his way to the restrooms in the back. There were a couple of girls who'd been eyeing him and the last thing he needed was them trying to get him to dance.

He didn't mind watching from a chair with a drink in his hand, but being out there gyrating around to the beat himself?

Nuh-uh. Not gonna happen.

Luckily, he made it all the way to the bathroom without being accosted. He took care of business and was headed back out into the noise and crowd when his gaze hit on a head of thick long red hair. The sight stopped him dead in his tracks even as his heart kicked into high gear.

Was CeCe here? Did she take that private jet of hers the boys had mentioned and follow him to the event? If she did, he would certainly oblige her in her quest to initiate him into the mile high club, should she ask.

Knocking himself out of his surprised stupor, he took the few long strides it took for him to get to her.

Grinning like a fool, he tapped her on the shoulder. "Fancy meeting you here."

When she turned, he realized his mistake. The stranger smiled wide. "Hey, there."

He saw immediately how wrong he'd been. She looked nothing like CeCe. This woman was shorter and she didn't have CeCe's willowy figure. Her outfit was too tight and too loud.

CeCe's clothes might have been seductive, but it was subtle and even a man like Wade could tell they were expensive and well made, fitting her like a glove.

"Um, sorry. I thought I knew you."

She reached out and touched his arm. "That's okay. You can get to know me."

He took a step back so she had to drop her hold on him. "I, uh, gotta get back to my friends."

Wade fled the scene like a coward. He supposed he was one, afraid of one woman and her flirting.

What the fuck was wrong with him? He hadn't come up with an answer to that question yet as he sidled around to the far side of his friends' table, back to the safety of his seat.

"The redhead blow you off?" Shorty grinned.

Damn guy was too observant.

"Yup." It was easier to lie than to explain that he'd willingly left the only redhead he was interested in back in California.

"Mind if I take a shot at her?" Clint asked.

Wade snorted at the request. "Not at all. Go ahead."

As he watched the stock handler work his way across the room, Wade could only hope Clint kept the woman on the other side of the bar. Wade obviously wasn't in the mood for female conversation tonight.

In fact, male conversation wasn't holding his attention too well at the moment either and he had a feeling he knew why. They weren't talking about CeCe—the only subject he was interested in.

Shit.

"So what're you doing after the event Sunday?" Shorty asked. "We got a couple weeks break."

"Yeah, I know." Those weeks off were going to seem interminable. Resisting the lure to head back to California and kill time in CeCe's big bed was going to kill him. "I might head back home. You?"

"I'm heading directly home. The wife's to do list, on top of my regular chores, will keep me busy for a couple of weeks, plus some." Shorty grinned and Wade felt the stab of jealousy.

The ranch was Wade's home. His granddaddy, his parents and his brother all lived on the property, though in their own houses.

Wade had a small house that his stuff occupied, even if he didn't get there very often. His daughter lived with his ex-wife a couple of towns over. He saw her when he could but she was a teenager now. She had better things to do than hang out with a father who was hardly ever around.

He had family at the ranch and he knew he always had a chair at the dinner table and a rack for his blanket and saddle in the barn, but it wasn't a home like Shorty had.

There was no little woman waiting on him. No kids to run out to the drive and greet him at the truck. He hadn't realized he wanted any of those things but the pang in his chest while listening to Shorty talk about them was unmistakable.

Wade knew of one way to get rid of aches and pains, of all

varieties. He reached for the whisky and downed it.

At the same time, Shorty reached for his cell phone. He frowned down at the read-out and let out a humph.

"What's up?" Wade asked.

"I just got a text. It looks like they're looking for bull fighters during the Lane Rodeo and Stock Sale next weekend. That's held right near your place, right?"

"Yeah, actually. Pretty close. You gonna work it?"

"I don't think I can. I told the wife I wouldn't take on anything next week. We promised the kids we'd go camping." Shorty glanced up. "You should do it. It's practically in your backyard and the pay's not bad."

"Hmm. Maybe I will."

"I'll forward you the text."

"Thanks." Wade nodded.

He might as well pick up some work. Two uninterrupted weeks at home loomed like an eternity to a man used to never being there. He'd need a break from his relatives for at least a couple of hours.

CHAPTER EIGHTEEN

Maggie came into the office and dropped a large envelope onto the corner of CeCe's desk. "This came for you."

She glanced at it and then to her assistant. "What's this?"

"I don't know. It came with the Fed Ex morning delivery." Maggie's answer wasn't all that informative.

Since the delivery company's name was written in bold blue letters across the white overnight mail envelope, CeCe had already guessed that.

She'd just have to open it up and find out. "All right. Thank you."

CeCe grabbed the envelope and glanced at the return address. It was from her lawyer. This couldn't be good. Then again, how bad could it be? The divorce was finalized months ago.

Frowning, she tore into the envelope and pulled out a cover letter attached to a document she recognized immediately.

The boat title John had brought over for her to sign last week.

The paper she should have just signed and been done with.

Instead, she'd made him send it through his lawyer to hers and the results would end up the same anyway. She'd sign the damn paper and both sets of lawyers got to add to their billable hours.

What the hell had she been thinking? She'd been stubborn and spiteful and the only one who benefited was their overpaid legal council.

Reaching for a pen, she signed the paperwork and shoved it into the envelope so Maggie could send it back. Maybe she'd have it couriered directly over to John today so he didn't have to wait for it any longer.

She might not love the man any more but she also didn't seem to hate him as much as she used to either.

That was progress.

It was kind of freeing, letting go of the anger. It was as if the bitter taste that overwhelmed everything for the past year had finally disappeared and she could enjoy the flavor of life again.

She stood and carried the envelope to Maggie's desk. "Is there someone who can drop this off at Mr. Cole's office today?"

"Yes, ma'am. I'll take care of it."

"Great. Thanks." CeCe turned to leave just as Maggie's phone rang.

Halfway back to her desk, she heard Maggie say, "Let me see if Ms. Cole is available."

CeCe paused and pivoted back to Maggie.

The girl punched the hold button and glanced up. "It's that bull rider charity you contacted."

"Oh, good. Put them through to my line." CeCe walked through the door of her office just as the phone started to ring. She reached across it and lifted the receiver. "This is CeCe Cole."

Sidling around the desk to the other side, she lowered herself into the chair as the voice in her ear said, "Mrs. Cole. This is Verna Parks—"

"From the charity. Yes. Thank you for getting back to

me."

The woman laughed "No, thank you for contacting us. We're overwhelmed by your offer."

CeCe smiled. "Not too overwhelmed, I hope."

"Not at all. We'd love to work with you and your company."

And her company's money, CeCe was sure, but that had been what she wanted when she'd made contact to give financial support to a worthy cause all while raising good will for Cole Shock Absorbers.

As a registered not-for-profit, the organization that helped injured bull riders would make good use of her funds.

"Actually—and I hate to ask because it's so last minute—but there is an event coming up next weekend that our organization will have a major presence at. I know how busy you are but if you were able and willing to attend—"

"No problem." CeCe cut off the woman's rambling. She knew what Ms. Parks was trying to ask in her very roundabout way. "Just tell me where and when and I'll be there."

"It's Saturday in Texas so I totally understand if it's too—"

"No problem at all." CeCe had the corporate jet so it wasn't as if she had to worry about booking a commercial flight.

"That would be amazing. Having a woman of your stature in attendance, honestly we never expected to be so lucky."

CeCe had already pledged the funding, so it wasn't as if Ms. Parks had to lay it on so thick. "As I said, I'm happy to pledge next year's charity budget to your organization."

"And we appreciate it. But it's so much more than the money. I'm not sure you understand how small and unknown we are. Obscurity is our biggest hurdle. Being overlooked makes fundraising on a wide scale even more difficult in an economy that is already painful for not-for-profits. You, Mrs. Cole, are a household name."

"Well, bearing the Cole last name does have its benefits."

One reason she hadn't ditched it.

"With all due respect, you were well respected in your own right long before you married into the Cole family."

That gave CeCe pause. In the face of the overwhelming Cole dynasty it was easy to forget the life she had before John. CeCe was perfectly genuine when she said, "Thank you, Ms. Parks. I appreciate you saying so." Clearing the emotion from her throat, CeCe continued, "I'll transfer you back to my assistant so you can give her the specifics for the event."

"Wonderful. See you soon."

"See you soon." CeCe punched the button to transfer the call and then replaced the receiver.

Making her own choices, slowly but surely changing things to please herself rather than her husband, she could feel that this was the right path to taking her life—and her identity—back.

Before she was Mrs. Cole she was CeCe Carlton and though there was no doubt she was more wealthy and powerful now than she'd been then, it didn't hurt to remember the past.

Just as Ms. Parks had reminded her, CeCe Carlton had commanded quite a bit of attention in her own right. It was time she remembered that.

Smiling, she went back to work on the massive amount of emails that had accumulated in her inbox.

Lost in cyberspace correspondence, she didn't know how long she'd been at it when the phone on her desk rang.

Happy for the break, she reached for it, assuming it was her assistant. "Yes."

"CeCe." The sound of her ex-husband's voice greeted her. That was a surprise.

"John." She frowned, wondering what the occasion was that he'd felt the need to call her.

"I just got back from North Carolina."

"All right." That still didn't explain much. There was a branch of Cole Auto Parts in Charlotte but it wasn't part of her holdings. "And?"

"I just—" John hesitated before he let out a breath. "I wanted to say thank you."

"For what?"

"For signing that boat title"

"John, it was in the divorce agreement that you got it. Why wouldn't I sign it?"

"I know, but thanks for handling it right away and getting it back to me so fast. I have a buyer for it and any delay might have cost me the deal."

She realized what he was getting at. "And I usually drag my feet."

"Well, yeah, it was what I was expecting."

She could have been mad at him for bringing up her shortcomings, all of which she was aware of but liked to ignore as often as possible.

Instead, CeCe lifted one shoulder. "I guess I don't like to be too predictable."

He laughed. "Anyway, thank you."

"You're welcome." She leaned back and rested her head against the chair, noticing for maybe the first time how confortable it was. "So you're selling the boat? I thought you loved it."

"I did. I do, but I'm upgrading. Getting one ten feet bigger."

Of course, he was. Bigger was always better with John. That was one reason why she was rambling around in such a huge home when one half the size would more than do.

"Ten feet. Wow." So many snarky comments ran through her head, at least one of which referred to overcompensating for the size of his penis, but she resisted the urge. "Good luck with it."

Odd. In past she never would have buried the impulse to point out that a longer boat did not in fact make a man's dick bigger.

"Thanks. So that's what I wanted to say. I'll let you go."

"Yeah, I should get going. I have a bunch of things I need to do. Apparently, I'm going to be at a rodeo in Texas this weekend. I suppose I should buy something more rodeo appropriate to wear finally since it looks like I'll be attending more."

"I thought the bull riding circuit was on a break this week."

"Oh, it is." She knew that because, for better or worse, she was keeping tabs on the professional bull riding circuit Wade worked. "This is some small event. I'm supporting one of the charities that helps injured cowboys. They asked if I could make an appearance."

"I'm impressed."

She laughed. "Are you? Why?"

"I'd always been under the impression you wanted nothing to do with the bull riding association sponsorship—other than to annoy me that your part of the company had it and mine didn't that is."

An unbidden laugh burst from CeCe at the truth of that. "It did start out that way. Now, I don't know. I guess I'm interested."

"It got you hooked, huh? Yeah, that's how it goes sometimes."

"I guess. So enjoy your boat."

"Thanks. Enjoy your rodeo."

"Thanks." CeCe hung up the call with her ex and for once, didn't feel like screaming or throwing something.

This was definitely progress and would probably save her from getting an ulcer. Or at least from getting frown lines from scowling.

It was no lie she'd told John. In spite of having a walk-in closet bigger than the size of Wade's hotel room, she did need to go shopping. She'd sacrificed enough heels to the arena dirt.

Time for a pair of good old cowboy boots like Wade's pair that had spent so much time on the floor of her bedroom.

Strangely, that memory made her smile and feel sad at the same time.

Standing, CeCe sighed. A couple of nights and Wade had

wiggled his way into her life and taken root.

What she was going to do about it was the question.

That was something she could—and likely would—worry about later.

Later, while she was alone in the dark in that big bed in her huge house, trying to, but not sleeping.

Enough wallowing. Right now, it was time to shop.

CHAPTER NINETEEN

Wade left his bag in the truck, since there was no locker room to stash it in at the open air arena.

He slammed the door of his truck and made sure in was locked. Pocketing the keys, he turned toward the entrance.

"Wade!" The familiar female voice had him turning and stifling a groan.

His ex-wife, Eve, stood across the parking lot. He recognized both her and the car he had paid for.

He should have known just from her name alone to not succumb to the temptations Eve had offered all those years ago.

Hadn't Adam paid a high price for the same weakness? Wade should have learned from Adam's biblical mistake, but he hadn't.

Instead Wade had ignored the hiss of the metaphorical snake when he'd given in to that night of passion in the bed of his truck nearly fifteen years ago.

The result of that night stood next to Eve now.

Brittany. His daughter.

No matter how bad things got with him and Eve, Wade would never regret having her. Brit loved him in spite of her mother trying to pollute her feelings toward him.

Having a vicious ex-wife and paying years of continuing child support—yeah, *that* he could have lived happily without.

He moved toward them since, apparently, Eve wasn't going to come to him. She had yet to move from the spot where she stood next to her car.

That was about right. Obstinate, as always. So much so she wouldn't even take a single frigging step to shorten his path to her.

Resigned, Wade hastened his pace. When he'd almost reached them, his daughter smiled and all his anger toward his ex faded away.

"Brittany."

"Hey, Dad." The lift in the corners of her mouth was a little bit crooked, just like his. She was his child, no doubt about it.

"Come here and let me hug you." He wrapped his arms around the girl and pressed a kiss to the top of her head, noticing she was now so tall he didn't need to bend to do that.

When had that happened? She'd apparently shot up when he wasn't looking. She was already as tall as her mother. If she kept growing she could end up as tall as Wade. For a female, that was damn tall.

Brittany, being a teenager, only put up with a short hug from him before she pulled back and rolled her hazel eyes.

"Dad. People are gonna think we're weird or something." She flung the end of one long braid, the same color as Wade's hair, as she looked embarrassed at his show of affection.

"They already think that about me." Taking pride that his family genes were strong enough to make his daughter look as much like him as she did his ex-wife, he shot Eve a glance. "Hey."

Not smiling, Eve responded, "Hey."

Not a whole lot of civility in that greeting, but no hostility either. That was about as good as he could expect, he supposed.

At least she'd done as he'd asked and brought Brittany to the event to see him. That was more than he'd assumed she'd do.

He decided to be the bigger person, if only to make her look like the smaller one. Though he supposed the good behavior on her part should at least be acknowledged. "Thanks for bringing her over."

Eve lifted one shoulder. "I got somewhere I need to be anyway so I'm leaving her here with you. You can drop her off at my place later."

So basically she was leaving a girl who'd just turned fourteen alone at the rodeo knowing Wade had to work it and wouldn't be able to keep an eye on her.

He was standing there in front of her in his jersey, shorts and sneakers, shin guards already on and everything. They'd been married long enough she knew he was there to work, not for fun.

Yeah, that was more like the Eve he knew, purposefully making his life more difficult whenever she had the chance. That was bad enough, but her leaving their daughter unsupervised at a public event was quite another.

This was a small town and a family friendly event, but there were also too many damn strangers who were just passing through for him to feel comfortable not having someone keep an eye on Brittany.

He'd figure something out. A couple of the riders had their wives and kids here today. He knew a few of them well enough he could ask them if Brittany could sit with them during the competition when he'd be in the arena working.

Of course, Eve couldn't have known that. He had asked if Brittany could come today to see him, so in Eve's mind it would no doubt be all Wade's fault.

Ah, the pleasures of divorce . . .

Annoyed and fighting anger, he ignored Eve and looped an arm around Brittany's neck. He forced the emotions down and smiled at his daughter. "You have everything you need from the car?"

"Yeah." She held up the tiny backpack-shaped bag in her hand before looping it over her shoulder.

"Okay. Let's get you settled before the show starts." He turned with her toward the performers' entrance. "You hungry? They have those foot-long corndogs you like."

"Dad, I'm on a diet."

He frowned at her. "A diet? You're fourteen."

"And I'm getting a fat belly."

"You are not. You're growing as fast as a filly. Your body needs fuel to do that and that means food."

They'd only taken a step when he heard, "Um, good-bye."

The annoyed tone in Eve's voice had him smiling for real now.

Brittany turned back. "Bye, Mom."

Without looking back, Wade lifted one arm in a move that would look like a goodbye, but in his mind was far more of a FU.

It was petty, but pissing off Eve was one of the small pleasures Wade treasured since the divorce. It made writing that check every month a little less painful. "How about we split one corndog. Then it's only half the calories. Sounds like a pretty good diet to me."

Brittany let out a noise, but finally he felt her shoulder drop in defeat. "Okay. But you have to promise to eat your half."

"I don't need to promise." He pulled her closer. "Just try and stop me from eating my half."

"Dad, I'm too big for hugs."

"If I'm not, you're not." Wade pressed a kiss to the top of her head. "Besides, nobody's ever too big for hugs."

He finally relented and let her go before she rolled her eyes so hard at him she gave herself a headache.

They made their way from the parking lot to the grounds where the pre-event activity was at a peak.

"I'll find you somebody to hang out with for while I'm working."

Her brow drew low in a viciously deep frown. "I don't

need a babysitter."

"I didn't say a babysitter. I said someone to hang out with."

"Same thing." Brittany scowled. "Mom let's me babysit the neighbor's kid now."

Wade cocked a brow. "Really?"

She spun to glare at him. "Yes. They pay me seven dollars an hour. Ask her."

In a defensive move, he held his hands up. "Okay. I believe she lets you babysit. But sitting inside a neighbor's house with your mamma right next door is one thing. Being in the stands of an arena crowded with strangers is another. Understand?"

"No." She pulled her mouth to the side.

"Well, too bad." Wade wasn't blind. He knew Brittany looked far older than she was.

More than a few guys turned to watch her pass by, even with Wade walking next to her. What the hell would they do if she were in the stands alone? He couldn't beat up every one of them, just as he couldn't be there with her every second at an event he was supposed to be working.

He sighed, longing for the days she was only knee high to him when he could toss her on his shoulders. Back then when folks said she was cute, he knew they were looking at her missing front tooth, not her budding breasts.

God help him, she was growing up too damn fast.

Chances were she'd turn out just fine. In spite of his feelings about her, he truly believed Eve was a good mother—but Brittany's teen years might just kill him, if worrying about her at today's event didn't do that first.

It didn't help he was already feeling a little unsteady over the CeCe situation.

Women usually didn't stick with him after he left them. Not like CeCe had.

Why was that? And what was he going to do about it?

He sure as fuck didn't have time to think about that now.

Maybe there was an upside to having Brittany with him

today. While he was busy worrying about his daughter, he didn't have time to obsess over missing CeCe.

That would be a nice change after the past week of doing exactly that.

CHAPTER TWENTY

The difference between cowboy boots and high heels was like night and day.

CeCe didn't sink in the dirt or the grass. She didn't have to worry her nine hundred dollar heels would get scuffed and ruined in the gravel parking lot.

Hell, her feet didn't even hurt. And snakeskin was virtually a neutral—the color would match just about anything she paired it with.

CeCe might have to consider wearing these things on a daily basis. At least while she was in Texas. The boots might earn her some strange looks in the office in California but here at the rodeo she fit right in.

"Mrs. Cole!"

CeCe turned at the sound of her name being called from a distance. She saw a squat, dark haired woman in jeans and boots hustling toward her. Venturing a guess, she had to assume this was the woman she'd spoken to on the phone from the organization.

The woman reached her, arm extended. "I'm Verna Parks. We spoke on the phone. I'm so happy you could make it."

"My pleasure." CeCe pasted on her public smile.

"We have the press here. They'd love to take a few pictures of you in the fundraising booth. If that's all right, of course. I'm sorry. I should have asked you first."

This time CeCe's smile was genuine. "Don't worry. Photos are fine."

As long as she was dressed, made up and looked good—all of which was true today—CeCe never objected to posing for pictures. In fact, she'd love to have a few of her in her new role as sponsor while wearing her rodeo-wear.

"Oh, good. Thank you. It will mean so much for our public relations."

"Of course. I understand completely."

"Let me show you were the booth is set up, then I can go grab the reporter so we can get the pictures out of the way. We wouldn't expect you to miss the show. We reserved a front row ticket for you."

"Thank you. That's very kind." CeCe didn't care all that much about watching the event.

This wasn't the circuit associated with the bull riding association that Cole's had sponsored, so she doubted any of the competitors she'd come to know would be here.

That was a good thing. Aaron wouldn't be here, or his girlfriend Jill with him. Or his friends, who she swore gave her strange looks last event.

Memories of that whole colossal mistake on her part had her stomach twisting, but they also led to thoughts of Wade.

Her belly tightened for a different reason as her body remembered the time spent with Wade.

Wade wouldn't be here either. It wasn't his usual circuit. That decreased her interest in watching this competition considerably. But she was here to support a worthy organization and that was what she intended to do.

Smiling, she turned toward the woman who was acting as her welcome committee. "Let's go do that interview, shall we?"

"Yes, ma'am. Right this way. It won't take too long. They're about to start the introductions, then there will be the opening ceremonies and you don't want to miss that."

"No, I certainly do not." CeCe hoped the sarcasm didn't come through in her tone.

"Mrs. Cole. This is John Shaw from the local paper."

"The local paper. How nice. Thank you for taking the time to cover this event." CeCe forced a smile.

"Our pleasure." He smiled back, looking genuinely pleased.

Her first thought was that there must not have been a little league game to fill the page in the sports section so they were running her interview. That was followed closely by the knowledge she needed to get a hold of her attitude.

She'd chosen this charity to sponsor. Smaller organization equaled smaller press, and that was exactly why she was here. To help them get exposure and more donations. But the moment she had the chance, she was putting her marketing department on this.

Poor Verna Parks and her organization obviously needed the help.

The local paper. CeCe stifled a groan.

"Maybe just stand to the left of the banner so we can read the organization's name."

She came back to reality at the sound of the reporter's suggestion. "Oh. Of course."

The reporter and photographer both stood by, watching, waiting as CeCe shifted to one side.

"Great. Perfect." The photographer raised the viewfinder to his face and CeCe's years of experience in front of a lens took over.

She smiled, comfortable again in the presence of the camera even if she wasn't used to being at the rodeo.

Although lately she seemed to be surrounded by dirt, large animals and cowboys more and more often—one of the results of stepping into John Cole's very large and smelly shoes.

The shutter snapped in rapid fire succession as CeCe made the slightest adjustments to her pose until finally the photographer lowered the camera. "I think we're good."

"Great." The reporter stepped forward, pad and pencil in hand. "A few questions?"

"Of course. Fire away." She flashed him teeth she knew were blindingly white after her last appointment with the cosmetic dentist.

"Can you tell us how you became aware of the organization? And what made you want to become a sponsor?"

"Sure." CeCe nodded and launched into the rote answer she'd prepared, the same one she'd given during the meeting to her PR and finance department.

At the same time the action around her ramped up. An announcer's amplified voice cut through the air, welcoming the attendees.

CeCe tried to focus in the midst of the noise reverberating off the stands the ticket holders occupied. She managed to get through her answer, but she had to lean in closer to the reporter and practically shout to do it.

As she waited to see if there would be any follow-up questions, the amplified announcer rambled on. "And the veteran among the bull fighters out on the dirt today, working personal security for us while the big show circuit is on a break, local Wade Long."

Hearing his name caught CeCe's attention.

Hell, it more than captured her full focus, it had her unable to concentrate on anything but the fact that Wade was here. Somewhere.

Heart pounding, she scanned the arena, searching for him with her gaze.

"Mrs. Cole?"

"Um, sorry. Can you repeat the question?" She forced herself to abandon her visual search and turn toward the reporter.

"I just asked if you have a background in rodeo? Did you attend as a child? Or perhaps ride yourself?"

The laugh came out short and unbidden. "No. I

discovered the sport late in life but I'm very glad I did."

He scribbled in his book and then glanced up. "Okay. Great. If I could contact you with any follow-up questions should they arise?"

"Of course."

"Great. Then we're done. Thank you very much for taking the time."

"Thank you." She shook his hand before saying, "I think I will go find my seat if you don't mind."

"Please do. And here is your ticket." Beaming, Ms. Parks handed her the small white ticket. "Do you need me to show you where—"

"No. I'm good. Thanks." The truth was CeCe was going to look for Wade, not her seat.

Ever grateful that the cowboy boots made it easier to navigate the grass and dirt, CeCe took advantage of the length of her legs as she strode toward the rail along the arena's perimeter. She couldn't get there fast enough. The need to see Wade overtook her.

It was insane, this desire to get to him. What was she going to do when she did? Certainly not admit she'd missed him to the point of distraction. But she wouldn't have to miss him tonight.

She'd worry about tomorrow later.

At the rail, she leaned against the metal and visually searched the area. She'd heard him introduced so he must be there somewhere . . .

And there he was.

Her heart pounded at the sight of Wade taking a lap around the arena. He jogged at a brisk pace, waving to the crowd with his straw cowboy hat.

She saw the moment he saw her. Wade did a literal double take. He glanced in her direction, turned away, and whipped his head back, eyes wide.

Given how sure of foot he usually was, it surprised her when he tripped to a halt.

He squinted in her direction for a moment, as if not

believing his eyes, before he strode toward her.

"CeCe?"

"Hi, Wade." She couldn't help her smile.

"Damn. Yours was the last face I expected to see in the crowd today." He laughed. "What are you doing here? Did you come looking for me?"

Her smile faded as quickly as it had come. "No. I didn't come looking for you. What? You think I'm stalking you or something? I'm here as a sponsor for the rider charity, you self-centered, obnoxious man."

The outburst more than likely stemmed from her guilt that she had done a fair amount of googling with Wade as the subject of her search. She'd told the therapist she was making progress being able to let Wade go, but there she was on the computer just hours later.

But in her defense, nowhere had it said he would be here today.

He tipped his head to the side, a cocky smirk on his face. He leaned in closer, bracing his forearms against the railing and shaking his head. "You couldn't let me be happy for just a few minutes believing you came looking for me? You are one hard woman, CeCe Cole. Beautiful, but hard."

She drew her brows down, digesting his words even as he grinned at her. Had he wanted her to come looking for him? "You were happy?"

"Yup." Wade drew the short word out in the slow, languid way she'd become used to him doing during their time together. "Happiest I've been in—about a week and a half or so."

"Oh." They'd been separated for about a week and a half, or close enough to it that she got his meaning.

Was he telling her, in his roundabout way, that he hadn't been happy since leaving her?

She was too damn old to play teenage games and guess at what he was feeling. Flirting was one thing—she enjoyed that—but games were another.

CeCe drew in a breath, about to tell him that, when he

climbed over the railing. She had to take a step back as his boots hit the ground.

He stood before her and treated her to his signature cocky grin. The one she didn't want to admit to him she'd missed seeing daily even if he could be the most frustrating and annoying man on Earth.

"Hey there, beautiful. I didn't get to give you a proper hello." Hands cupping her face, Wade leaned in and pressed a kiss to her lips.

She felt the rough scrape of stubble against her face and remembered how he only shaved every other day. Today must be the off day. She tasted the mint of the gum he was chewing. She knew it was because he tried to not chew tobacco during the actual event, only allowing himself to before and after.

Every thought careening through her brain while his lips pressed to hers made her realize how much she'd come to know about the man after only having been with him for a short time.

That was the last thought she had before he broke off the kiss, much too quickly in her opinion. Pulling back, he glanced at the stands behind her. He shook his head and stifled a cuss, dropping his hands away from her.

"What's wrong?" She missed the heat of the contact immediately.

"I can't do this here." His disappointing words were accompanied by the slow sway of his head.

"Do what? Kiss me?"

The regret, obvious in his expression was some consolation. "Yup. Not even a little bit, 'cause there ain't nothing little about what I feel when it comes to kissing you."

"Really?"

As a crooked smile tipped up one corner of his mouth higher than the other, Wade shook his head. "Yeah, really, and you damn well know it. You're too damn tempting. And I'm supposed to be working. Not to mention that there's someone here watching who shouldn't see me acting like a horny teenaged boy around you."

The attraction to him that had tightened her belly was replaced by nausea.

Was the bastard married? Or did he have a serious girlfriend and she was here? How dare he kiss her.

"Who's here?" She spun to search the crowd for the woman Wade had two timed while in her bed.

"Retract your claws, beautiful. It's not another woman."

"I never thought it was—"

She didn't get to finish her denial as Wade interrupted, "Yeah, you did. And it's my daughter."

"Your daughter?" That concept stole anything else she might have thought to say. Her anger was replaced with curiosity. "She's here?"

"Yup." He tipped his head toward the stands. "See the girl in the pink tank top with the braided hair?"

"*That's* your daughter?" CeCe hadn't known what she expected but it hadn't been the young woman Wade had pointed out.

"Yes, ma'am. That's Brittany. God help me." He let out a breath that sounded as if he was weary. "God, I wish the temperature would drop like forty degrees so maybe she'd put on a sweater."

There wasn't much chance of Wade getting his wish. The Texas sun was still high in the sky, beating its heat down on everyone.

CeCe glanced at the girl, taking note of all the details that added to her perfection. Most likely the same things that made Wade, as a father, sound so exhausted.

Her long willowy arms, in perfect proportion with her tall slim body. The graceful curve of her neck, the upturn of her nose. High cheekbones set off by a mane of thick hair contained in a braid that reached to her elbow.

"She's breathtaking."

He sighed. "Yup, for better or worse, she's a beauty. Just like her mother."

The comment had CeCe shifting her attention. She moved from Brittany, who had no idea she was under scrutiny while she chatted with the much younger boy standing beside her, to Wade. "You told me your ex-wife was a bitch. You never told me she was beautiful."

"Oh, she is both. A beautiful bitch." Wade lifted a brow and shot CeCe a look. "Apparently, I have a type."

CeCe scowled and said without humor, "Ha, ha."

"Keep that temper of yours in check, beautiful. You know how I love when you get riled up. I might not be able to control myself." He smiled and winked.

She'd risen to the bait, as she always did with Wade. He knew exactly how to push her buttons.

Not giving him the satisfaction of a response, she changed the subject back to his daughter. "You know, with her height she could be a model."

His eyes widened. "Over my dead body, she will."

"Why? I modeled."

"That's fine. I'm not your father. I am hers. She's only just turned fourteen."

CeCe saw the genuine concern in him. "This is a new side of you. Over protective father."

"Nothing over protective about it. It's common sense. I was a boy once. I know how they think. And believe me, I don't want any males thinking about my daughter like that."

She knew first hand how Wade thought, especially when it came to sex. She couldn't say she blamed him for worrying about boys thinking similar things about his daughter. Though it was amusing to see this side of him.

CeCe glanced at the beautiful girl again before turning back to Wade. "What happened between you and her mother?"

He lifted his brows, as if surprised she'd asked. After throwing a quick glance over his shoulder at the arena, which was filling with a stream of young women on horseback, he looked back to CeCe. "They're gonna bring the colors in any second. Then there'll be the National Anthem and the opening prayer. Then it's show time. I don't have a whole lotta time to talk right now."

"Will it take a long time to answer my question?"

"No. I guess not. We were young. We—or at least I—never intended it to last longer than a few tumbles. Maybe the summer. Sorry to be crude but it's the truth." His gaze met hers. "Then Brittany came along and changed all that."

So he'd gotten married because she'd been pregnant.

"And if you'd all rise for the presentation of the stars and stripes . . ." The announcer's request put an end to a more in depth discussion at the moment, just as Wade had predicted.

Wade shot CeCe a look. "Good enough explanation?"

"Yes. Thank you for telling me."

"Anytime." After one more look that felt ripe with meaning, he turned to face the arena.

A girl on horseback rode around the perimeter at breakneck speed. Her hair streamed behind her nearly as far reaching as the red and white stripes on the flag she carried.

CeCe took a step forward and stood next to Wade, shoulder to shoulder with him as he took off his hat and held it over his heart. He held it there through the singing of the National Anthem, and then bowed his head throughout the blessing of the event, the participants and the animals.

The opening ceremony finished with an audible, "Amen" from the crowd, echoed by Wade.

Having been more intrigued with the man next to her than what was happening out on the dirt, CeCe mumbled the same and then watched as he planted his hat back on his head.

"I gotta get out there. You'll be here for the whole thing until the end?" he asked.

"Yes." She had been considering sneaking out early and taking the car to the airport where her jet was on standby to leave tonight. That plan had gone out the window the moment she heard Wade's name over the loudspeaker.

"Good." He smiled. "You have a seat?"

She had yet to look at where that seat was, but she had a ticket. She held it up for Wade now. "Yes."

He nodded. "Okay. I'll see you when I'm done. Maybe we can grab a bite after?"

"I'd like that."

"It's a plan then." His grin had her heart fluttering.

He slid on sunglasses but she felt the power of his gaze even after she was no longer able to see his eyes.

Damn. She was in trouble with this man.

He turned toward the fence and only after he'd vaulted over it did she turn toward the stands.

First, she'd find her seat. Then she'd call the pilot and tell him she'd be flying out later than she'd thought. Possibly even tomorrow rather than today.

Sometimes being the owner of Cole Shock Absorbers, and the Cole jet, had its benefits.

"Excuse me." She tapped a man wearing an official-looking shirt on the shoulder. When he turned to face her, she thrust the ticket forward. "Can you tell me where this is?"

The older man squinted at the ticket and nodded. "Yes, ma'am. That's this section right over there. Front row."

He tipped his chin in the direction of the section where Wade had pointed out Brittany. After a closer look, CeCe saw the empty spot next to her. She thanked the man and made her way over. A second check of her ticket and the number marked on the section proved that was the place.

It looked as if CeCe and Wade's daughter would be spending some time together. That was an intriguing and kind of frightening concept for a woman who had no children of her own.

CeCe took her place next to Brittany and couldn't help glancing over.

The girl must have felt CeCe's gaze on her. She turned her head and said, "Hey."

"Hey." CeCe answered her in kind.

"You know one of the riders?" she asked.

"Um, no. I don't think I know any of the riders." That wasn't a lie. Wade wasn't riding. "Why do you ask?"

Brittany lifted one shoulder. "No reason. It's just that this section is usually where the riders' families sit."

"Oh. Well, I contributed to the relief organization so one of the people from the booth gave me this ticket."

In exchange for the check with a whole lot of zeroes on it that she'd had the finance department cut to the organization . . . CeCe didn't mention that detail to Brittany.

"Oh." Another lift of one shoulder from Brittany was followed by, "That's cool."

CeCe guessed she passed the test and would be allowed to stay in the *family* section. Meanwhile, the fact she was sitting and talking to Wade's daughter, peeking into a part of his life she never knew existed until today, made the whole day feel even more surreal.

Seeing him as a father was beyond strange. She'd known him as an overt flirt and a cocky smartass. She'd seen him drunk and in the throes of passion. But never had she even thought to imagine him in the role of concerned father.

It gave her something to chew on while the first event began.

She'd never had kids of her own but technically she wasn't completely out of the realm of motherhood. She was a stepmother to John's son from his first marriage, but the first Mrs. Cole had custody.

During their marriage, CeCe had only seen the boy a couple of times a year, and that was usually at some exotic vacation at an island resort or something equally distracting that John would insist on taking them all to for the times he had visitation.

Now, Johnny was an adult, off on his own, using his Masters Degree to build a career.

Sitting next to Brittany watching a rodeo was more than she'd ever done with her own stepson in all the years she'd been married to John. It made her feel closer to Wade and a little freaked out at the same time.

This was what normal felt like. It was strange.

Not unpleasant. Not at all. Just . . . different. Now that she'd tasted it, she wanted to try more. Wanted more of this with Wade. With his daughter too if he let her.

That fact scared CeCe, but that Wade might not give her the chance scared her even more.

Franticly searching until she found him again in the arena, CeCe went back to tracking Wade with her eyes.

She was definitely in trouble.

CHAPTER TWENTY-ONE

This being a small town charity rodeo might not be *the big leagues,* as the announcer had put it, but that didn't mean that Wade didn't have to be on the ball.

When he wasn't working to protect the bull riders, he was still in the arena. He was there just in case anything went wrong with the bareback or saddle bronc riders that the pickup man couldn't handle. He untied the calves during the tie-down competition. He even helped put the five-year old girls and boys on the sheep for the mutton bustin'.

There was downtime now and again between the individual events and his duties, but not enough for Wade to run over to see either his daughter or the woman who had his body on high alert.

Seeing the two were sitting next to each other made his decision to not try and talk to them until the event was over even easier. There definitely wasn't time to explain to Brittany who CeCe was, if he even could explain that to his daughter without revealing too much about their history.

Hell, explaining who CeCe was to Brittany would require Wade know what CeCe was to him first. He hadn't quite figured that out yet. He'd wondered about it though, pretty much on a daily basis since leaving her in California.

Wade didn't go over, but he watched them whenever he could, catching a glimpse here and there. He'd glanced over at one point to see them talking. The curiosity nearly had him vaulting over the rail and trotting over.

What the hell could they be chatting about? Him? Modeling? He found neither option comforting. Quite the opposite. Disturbing was a more accurate description.

Two hours passed with Wade trying to keep an eye on Brit and CeCe while working the rodeo. It was like trying to fight a battle that had two fronts, when just his job should have had his undivided attention.

Finally—amazingly—he made it to the final event without having gotten himself or anyone else hurt or killed. He just had to get through the bull riding. Then he could—what? Introduce the two females who'd had him on edge all day? Take them both to eat?

CeCe and Brittany, at the same table of the diner in Wade's hometown. That was an interesting idea. Scary as hell, but interesting.

This little corner of the world was where he'd grown up. Where Brit had been born. Where his ex-wife and his own family still lived.

Where even a whisper of news caused a wave of gossip among the locals that rippled throughout the town.

"Wade!" The sound of Lucky, one of the two other bullfighters, calling him broke Wade out of his deep thoughts.

"Yeah?" Wade turned.

Lucky was standing a few yards away. The three—Wade and his two fellow bullfighters—were already in formation in anticipation of the bull riding. They stood ready, spread out in a triangle with one man on each corner for the best coverage of the action about to happen.

"Just a heads up. The first bull is a real ball buster."

"Aren't they all?" Wade snorted.

Lucky tipped his head to the side. "You'll see. But this rider is good. He can handle him."

Wade glanced at the chute in which a little muley had been loaded. Eyeing the bull, with its short legs and no horns, he had to wonder about the validity of Lucky's warning.

The rider he'd referred to was straddling the rails above the chute, about to lower himself onto the bull.

Everybody in the area—those milling around behind the chutes, the other competitors, the stock owners, the rodeo personnel—all stopped what they were doing to watch the ride. That told him a lot.

On the circuit Wade worked, he'd only seen the arena go still for the best. The one percent of riders who guaranteed a great ride every time they got on the back of a bull.

When a rider was extra good, or a bull real rank, everyone in the know paused to take notice. When the two came together in one ride, history could be made.

Maybe Lucky was right about this match up. Wade took a step closer, his focus completely on the chute.

The animal reacted to the rider's weight on his back. The bull was a real chute buster. It was as if it was trying to knock the chute apart, kicking out behind him before rearing up in front.

In spite of the challenge the bull presented, the rider made progress getting ready for his ride. He took his wrap and immediately shifted forward, getting up close to his rope.

He eased his legs down and the bull's bad behavior increased but Lucky had been right that this guy was a veteran and knew how to handle himself in the situation.

Even though there was no way the bull was going to settle down and let him get in perfect position, the rider nodded his head to the gateman.

He got the hell out of the chute, fast, quick and in a hurry because any rider knew being in the chute with a bull misbehaving like this one was the most dangerous place to be.

The moment the gate swung open the bull turned out and to the left, spinning into the rider's hand.

Horns or not, the little muley proved he was one hell of a

bucker, but the rider did what he was supposed to do.

He kept his chin down, his eyes focused on the back of the bull's head, his free arm out and in front of him. He pivoted at the hips to absorb the power of the bull's jumps.

A mastery of the basic skills. Textbook perfect form. That's what made a rider be able to cover even the toughest bulls and if he could hang on for eight seconds, would earn him a damn nice score.

It was one hell of a ride. The rider held on until the buzzer sounded.

In position in case the kid got hung up, Wade bounced on the balls of his feet, prepared to move in.

The rope released and the rider leapt off on the outside of the spin, landing on his feet, before falling to his knees.

He half limped, half ran away from the danger zone as the bull stopped bucking and turned in a slow circle.

The animal knew who it was who rode him. In an arena with three bullfighters and a mounted safety man, the damn bull picked out the rider and took off after him.

The rider's limp disappeared as the bull went after him, sending him leaping for the rails to get up high and out of the way in a move that literally saved his ass.

Wade shouted to the bull, waving his hat to try and draw the animal's attention.

When the bull saw he couldn't get to the rider, and that the out gate was open wide and waiting for his exit, he took off at a trot. Without a backward glance, the bull headed for the back where he knew he'd find his feed bucket and some nice shavings to lay down in.

These animals weren't as dumb as most people thought. Even so, it was nice to see this bout was done.

After planting his hat back on his head, Wade stooped down and grabbed the bull rope that had fallen off the bull shortly after the rider jumped off.

The rider hopped down off the rails. A visible limp returned as he walked toward Wade to retrieve his rope.

"You a'ight?" Wade glanced down at the leg the man

favored. He could see every step was an effort.

The pain was clear in the rider's expression.

"Bull pinned my leg in the chute. Right on my bad knee." Gasping for breath, the rider had trouble getting out even those two sentences.

Wade glanced at the scoreboard. "Well, you're in first place now. That help that knee feel any better?"

Still breathing as if he'd run a marathon, the rider let out a short laugh. "Yeah. Little bit."

"Thought so." A paycheck at the end of a tough event always did make the riders feel better. Grinning, Wade slapped the guy on the shoulder. "Good ride, bud."

"Thanks." The kid limped his way to the riders' out gate as Wade had to think one more time how he had the better job.

Both professions had risk, yeah, but at least his had a guaranteed paycheck at the end of the night. And Wade's career in the pros hadn't ended in his early thirties like it did for so many riders in the higher level of the sport.

Aches and pains aside, it was a pretty nice gig. And speaking of gigs, this one was not over yet. Wade trotted back to his spot to get into position for the next ride.

This being a smaller rodeo, there were only a half a dozen more bull riders to go and they went fast.

Soon, Wade was done with his responsibilities—at least his responsibilities to his employer for the day. His duties regarding his daughter were another matter.

"Dad!" And here she came, headed in his direction.

And then there was CeCe . . . She trailed a few feet behind Brittany, looking uncertain.

His worlds were about to collide, if they hadn't already while the two had sat next to each other for the past two hours.

"Hey, baby girl." Wade wrapped his arm around his daughter's shoulders. "Did you meet CeCe?"

"CeCe?" Brittany turned big, innocent eyes up to him.

"That's me." CeCe took another step toward them.

Brittany drew her brows low. "You said you didn't know

anybody."

"No. You asked if I knew any of the riders, which I don't. You didn't ask if I knew one of the bullfighters."

Brittany's eyes widened at CeCe's answer and Wade decided he had better nip any potential conflict over the misunderstanding in the bud. He could always diffuse tension with a joke. "You have to be specific with CeCe. She's a city girl."

"I know. That's why I'm surprised. I figured she'd call you a rodeo clown like most city people. But she used the right word." There was a dusting of admiration in Brittany's tone and Wade couldn't be happier.

Call it a crazy hope, on so many levels, but he'd be thrilled if CeCe and Brittany got along. Of course, that depended on CeCe wanting to stick around for a while.

As she frowned and crossed her arms, he had to wonder if she would. "How did you know I was from a city?"

"You really have to ask that question?" Wade snorted as both he and his daughter sent CeCe a look of disbelief.

CeCe scowled. "I guess not."

He couldn't help but smile. "So, you want to grab some dinner before I drive you back to your mother's place?"

"Mom said to come right home."

Of course she did. Why give Wade any extra time with his own daughter?

He sighed. "Okay. I'll take you straight home then." But he intended on taking the long way. "CeCe?"

She lifted one perfect red brow. "Yes?"

"Would you like to take a ride with me to drop off Brit and then grab a bite after?" After being away from her for over a week, he'd like to both grab and bite CeCe.

She pursed her lips together and he could see her deciding. "I can do that. I just have to make a call. The pilot's waiting for me to tell him when we'll be leaving."

"It's getting pretty late. Why don't you tell him you'll leave tomorrow morning?" There was so much more behind Wade's question. So much he couldn't say in front of

Brittany. He hoped CeCe would hear the unspoken plea.

Stay.

For the night. For much longer than that but he'd settle for tonight.

Her blue gaze met and held his. After a pause, she nodded. "You're right. Tomorrow would be better."

"Wait. You have your own pilot?" Brittany's shocked question broke the tension.

CeCe smiled. "He came with the jet."

"Whoa. Are you serious?" Brittany's surprised gaze moved from CeCe to Wade.

"Believe me. It's true. Come on. We can talk about it in the truck." He loved his daughter, but today he was looking forward to dropping her off so he could welcome CeCe to Texas properly.

Today with CeCe had been an unexpected but welcome gift. He was going to grab it and hold on with both hands for as long as she'd let him.

CHAPTER TWENTY-TWO

Brittany waved good-bye from the door of her mother's house. The front door had barely closed when Wade threw his truck into gear, burning rubber as he peeled down the road and around the corner.

There he parked and turned toward CeCe. Pulling her toward him, he crashed his mouth into hers and kissed her the way he'd wanted to since first seeing her leaning against the rail at the rodeo.

God, she'd been a welcome sight. Like a mirage in the desert, her red hair a halo of gold beneath the glare of the afternoon sun.

He hadn't believed it was her. He'd had false alarms before where he'd imagined he'd seen her only to be disappointed.

But this time she was very real. Her lips against his, her body beneath his hands, were proof of that.

Wade pulled away from the kiss to say, "Damn, I missed you."

"I missed you too." Her breathless confession, on top of the high he was riding from the kiss, had Wade ready to tear her clothes off right there in the truck.

"Good." He groaned as he raked both his hands and his gaze down her body. "You have a hotel room?"

"No. I can get one—"

"No, you will not. You're coming home with me."

"Home with you?"

"Yup. To the ranch."

Her eyes widened. "Won't your family be there?"

"Don't worry, beautiful. I have my own house far enough away from the others ain't nobody gonna hear you. No matter how loud we get." He grinned. Not wanting to waste any more precious time, he put the gear into drive.

"You have your own house?"

"I do." He loved that she was interested, but he'd far rather have this conversation naked and in his bed, preferably after a nice long round of sex.

Though he'd wanted her so much since he'd seen her last, he doubted he'd last long at all.

With the image of CeCe in his bed, Wade broke a few speed limits as he headed for the ranch.

"So how big is it?" she asked.

"Oh, darlin', you know the answer to that." He shot her a sideways glance just in time to catch the face she made at him.

"I meant how big is the ranch?"

"Oh, that." Wade smirked. "About twenty-five thousand acres or so."

"Twenty-five *thousand* acres?" Her mouth fell open.

Wade shook his head at her reaction. "Spoken like a true city girl. You can't raise a decent-sized herd of cattle on much less than that."

What she probably didn't realize is that all those thousands probably cost less than her place with its postage stamp of a yard.

That was okay. He could educate her about everything she needed to know about ranching . . . and a few other things.

He'd gladly teach her all kinds of things. They'd only scratched the surface during their time together.

God, what he wouldn't give to have more time with her now. "Do you have to leave tomorrow?"

She angled her position in the passenger seat so she faced him. "Why?"

"I thought, maybe . . ." Why was this so hard? It shouldn't be. He sighed and opted for something he didn't usually go for. Complete and total honesty. "I'm not ready for you to leave so soon."

She was silent for long enough he glanced in her direction, holding his breath, afraid of what he'd see in her expression. What he saw was hesitation, but if he wasn't completely mistaken, she was tempted to stay.

Finally, CeCe asked, "What would your family say?"

He let out a short laugh. "I really don't care."

"But I do."

"I'm sorry. I know you do." He drew in a breath. "I don't think they'll care."

"Why not? Because you bring home so many women?"

He heard the jealousy clearly in her tone and damned if it didn't make him want to pull over and take her right there in the passenger seat.

"No. Not at all." He didn't like to have women in his home.

It made it too easy for them to assume things. Like that they'd be there a lot more than he wanted them there. Funny how he couldn't get CeCe there fast enough and he was starting to suspect he'd be damned happy if she never left. He pushed that thought, which was much too deep for here and now, aside.

"The truth is, I'm not around as much as the family thinks I should be."

"You're traveling for work though. Right?"

"Yup. And that's the problem. After my choosing to work the pro circuit rather than dedicate my entire life to the ranch full time, I think they kind of stopped caring what I do."

"I'd love to see your home." CeCe laid her hand on his thigh.

The heat of her hand penetrated the thin fabric of the shorts he hadn't taken the time to change out of after the rodeo.

"And I'd love to show it to you." Especially his bed. But they couldn't stay in his bed the entire time where he could easily distract her. What would she think of the rest of his place?

The famous model millionaire, CeCe Cole, in his little ranch house . . . This was going to be interesting.

Good thing he'd cleaned up before he'd left this morning. Still, no amount of cleaning was going to make it compare to her place.

Oh well.

At least he knew she liked him for him and not for what he owned—what little of that there was.

Had there ever been two more different people?

He had to be crazy to think he could hold on to her for more than a night or two.

"I'm excited to see the cows." She left her hand on his leg and squeezed. "Ooo, are there horses too?"

Wade raised a brow. Maybe he wasn't so crazy after all.

CHAPTER TWENTY-THREE

"Close your mouth, city girl, or bugs are gonna fly in."

Out of the corner of her eye, CeCe saw Wade shoot her a sideways glance and a grin as he steered the truck onto the drive for his family's ranch.

The entrance gates might have been made of wood rather than wrought iron like the houses in her neighborhood, but CeCe hadn't been able to keep her mouth from gaping as she saw his family's place.

Meanwhile, he had acted as if it was nothing.

Only twenty-five thousand acres, he'd said. *Can't raise a decent herd on less than that*, he'd said.

Maybe she was a city girl, but this wasn't what she'd expected from a man who, the night she'd met him, had been staying in a hotel that cost less a night than she paid to get a pedicure.

Frowning, she turned toward him and shook her head in confusion. "Why didn't you tell me you owned all this?"

"I don't own it. My eighty-year-old grandfather does." He cocked one brow high. "And thank God for that or my ex-wife would have owned half after the divorce."

Wade made a sharp right down a dirt road that came into

view shortly after they'd driven through the gates. He drove slowly, maneuvering over bumps and around dips in their path. All the while, the truck's tires kicked up a cloud of dust behind them.

A couple of minutes later, a building came into view. CeCe squinted through the haze to make it out in the distance. The closer they got, the more details she could distinguish.

The building was small, but in a charming sort of way. A saltbox roof slanted down over a covered front porch where two wooden rocking chairs sat.

The yellow house with white trim was surrounded by mature foundation plantings and larger trees that would no doubt cast a nice shade and protect from the worst heat of the day. That told her this was an older building, though it looked very well kept.

He stopped the truck in front and cut the engine. After unhooking his seatbelt, Wade turned in his seat. "So this is it. What do you think?"

"I love it."

"You do?" he asked.

"Yes." It was unexpected but not at all in a bad way.

"Well, I seriously hope you're not going to be after me for my money now that you've seen my family's spread." He cocked up one brow, but his serious act broke when a smile tipped up his lips.

"Don't worry. I'm not after your *spread*." CeCe unhooked her seatbelt as well, turning to face him more fully.

Nothing about her attraction to Wade made sense. Even if he had owned the twenty-five thousand acres himself, it wouldn't make their situation any more logical. She was a city girl living in California. He was a country boy from Texas.

On top of their many differences, their lives were separated by thousands of miles between them.

The millions of dollars separating them was pretty far down the list of why there was no way they should be together. The money probably came somewhere after the reality that they both had disastrous marriages in their pasts.

157

Only superseded by the fact they had absolutely nothing in common—except for in bed, of course.

Then there was the decade difference in their ages that she was conveniently ignoring.

"Well, that's good because my father and brother are probably going to inherit it all anyway. I'll count myself lucky if I'm even in the will."

"That's okay. I'm actually after you for the sex." Joking seemed CeCe's best course of action in this conversation, which had taken on a strangely serious undertone.

She reached out and ran a finger over the jersey covering his chest before she glanced down to the shorts and fluorescent sneakers. "And for your keen fashion sense, of course."

His gaze dropped to take in her finger as she snaked it beneath the fabric of his shorts and trailed one nail along the bare skin of his leg. "Thank you, but it's about time I got out of my work clothes. Come on inside."

"All right." Her voice sounded breathy to her own ears.

Damn man.

She wouldn't admit he literally took her breath away, but she would concede she wanted him, more than she ever had any other man in her life.

Why was that?

Wade opened his own door and then ran around the nose of the truck. He had her door open before she'd had time to gather up her purse. He was still acting the gentleman.

"So no one else lives here with you?" she asked when he'd offered her his hand.

"Just me. It was the house my grandfather built right after he and my grandmother got married. When they had kids, he decided to build a bigger one farther from the road. My father built his house close to that one. My brother built himself a place on the other side of the property." Wade shrugged. "This one was empty and starting to fall apart. I guess it wasn't good enough for any of them to want to bother with, so I decided to make it mine."

It was a crazy yet amazing tale.

Her grandparents had died when she was young and she didn't speak to her parents much. Not since she'd been a teenager and broke away from them, replacing her father as her manager.

That was a time in her life she didn't like to remember.

Luckily for her, Wade was here to help her forget. Standing on the front porch, he opened the front door, grabbed her hand and pulled her inside.

The living room had what looked like hand-hewn beams in the ceiling and wide board flooring. It was construction that would be hard to duplicate today.

She took a step forward and laid her hands on his chest, even as she glanced around her. "I like your house. There's history here. It's good you saved it."

"Glad you approve." He settled his hands on her hips.

"I do. I want a tour."

He backed her up, moving them both slowly down a narrow hallway. "Okay. How about I show you the bed first."

"If you do that, it will be a long time before we get to the rest of the house."

He lowered his head closer to hers. "Is that a problem?"

"No, I'm just surprised. A bed has never been a requirement for you before. Not in the truck, or the elevator, or in my kitchen."

"Yeah, well, that's not going to work here. My family has a tendency to waltz in unannounced. My brother doesn't deserve to see what I consider mine." His gaze dropped to the buttons of her shirt as he deftly worked to unfasten them while still walking her backward.

She drew in a sharp breath. "Yours? Really. So now I'm your property?"

"God, I love it when you're pissed off at me." His eyes narrowed before he crashed his mouth against hers.

Eyes closed from the intensity of the kiss, CeCe didn't see the room or the bed they tumbled onto. She only felt the bounce of the mattress beneath her and the weight of Wade's body on top of her.

She smelled freshly laundered pillowcases combined with Wade's scent. It made her crave his bare skin against hers on top of the smooth, cool cotton.

Blindly, she reached between them, unfastening the remaining buttons on her shirt, intent on finishing the job he'd started and get them both naked.

He pulled his mouth off hers. "You call that pilot?"

Breathless and needy, she didn't know why he'd chosen to start a conversation now. "Yes."

"When did you tell him you're leaving?" he asked.

"Tomorrow. Noon." CeCe couldn't stay longer.

For one, she had a company to get back to. More than that, she had nothing more with her than what was in her purse. Luckily she didn't tend to travel light, and inside that bag she had her cosmetics bag, dental floss and a toothbrush. She'd be doing the walk of shame tomorrow, going home in the same clothing she'd arrived in, but at least she'd have fresh breath and makeup on.

"Good enough, I guess." Wade drew in a deep breath, sending his nostrils flaring. "We'll just have to make the most of tonight . . . and tomorrow morning."

Feeling his hard length pressing into her as he lowered his mouth to hers again, CeCe was totally on board with that plan.

When his tongue stroked against hers, she started to think about calling the pilot and pushing that departure to a later time. Maybe another day even.

When he finally slid his sheathed length inside her and her body bowed off the bed, pure relief warred with the need for more.

Still kissing her, Wade pushed deeper and groaned, low and deep in his chest.

She felt the vibration rumble from his body through hers and she feared she might not want to leave at all.

CHAPTER TWENTY-FOUR

CeCe was trying to catch her breath, but the dryness in her throat wasn't helping her effort.

She tried to swallow and realized she had no saliva to do so. "Wade, I have to get up. I'm thirsty."

"I have no idea why." Wade grinned down at her and finally rolled to the side so his weight no longer held her captive beneath him. "There's water bottles in the fridge. I'm gonna take a quick shower. Feel free to join me."

He stood and winked at her, obviously ignoring the fact he was as naked as the day he was born, but a lot bigger . . . and still partially erect.

She'd better get the water fast.

Knowing Wade, and for better or worse she did know him, her time to rest between rounds was limited.

She wasn't quite as comfortable as he was padding around his house naked. Especially after what he'd said about his family popping in. CeCe grabbed Wade's jersey off the floor.

One look at it, and the dirt and dust on it, had her dropping it back to the floor where she'd gotten it. She moved to the dresser and, feeling equally guilty as she was curious, pulled open the top drawer and peered inside.

Socks. All in pairs, rolled and lined up with impressive neatness.

Closing that one she opened the next. Underwear.

One more drawer yielded a stack of neatly folded T-shirts. She pulled one out and held it up beneath her chin.

It fell to far above her knee.

Deciding it would cover enough, especially considering she was only running to the kitchen for a bottle of water, she pulled it over her head.

Her pilfering his clothes had yielded one surprise. Wade was surprisingly organized.

Another thing had been revealed—his room held little to nothing personal.

She considered what that meant as she strode barefooted over the cool floors of the hallway and toward the kitchen.

There was one obvious reason why the house was so neat and clean but didn't feel lived in. Wade traveled a lot. But she knew from her own travel that when she arrived home, the house became a shambles of suitcases, laundry and toiletries.

Of course, she traveled a bit heavier than Wade, luggage-wise, but the fact remained he lived more like this was a hotel than a home.

This man was not the kind to ever settle down if he didn't even do so in his own house.

She swung open the door of the fridge and reached inside. After grabbing two bottles from the shelf that didn't contain much else she turned . . . and nearly dropped the water in her hand.

The man, whose bulk filled the doorway where he'd stopped, resembled Wade enough that she didn't scream, but the sound was very close to the surface. One consolation was that he looked as surprised to see her standing there as she was to see him.

"Who are you?" he asked.

She lifted her brows in surprise at the gall of his question. "I could ask you the same thing."

In her own defense she had been invited inside by Wade.

This guy hadn't even knocked. If he had, she didn't hear it.

"I'm Wade's brother." He moved farther into the room and leaned against the edge of the heavy wooden table, crossing his arm over his chest.

He hadn't provided a name. Neither would she. "And I'm Wade's guest."

It was an obvious stand off and she was enjoying the cat and mouse, until his gaze dropped down to her exposed legs. He slowly raked his eyes back up to her face and let out a snort of a laugh.

"Yeah. I'm sure you are." A crooked smile, so like Wade's except she didn't find it at all attractive on this guy, tipped up the corner of his mouth. "So where'd he find you? Today's rodeo, I assume."

"You assume correctly. He did indeed find me there." She forced a smile she didn't feel. "Why do you ask? Jealous?"

"Pfft. Hardly. If I had a dollar for every buckle bunny my brother picked up thanks to his big time TV bull-fighting career, I'd be a rich man."

It was meant to wound her, and truth be told it did sting, but she wasn't about to let this asshole see that.

No wonder Wade didn't like coming home. It was more than obvious his brother had a bad case of envy. He was stuck here working the family ranch while Wade's career was televised as he traveled the country.

That still didn't excuse this man's rudeness to her or his ire toward Wade. He didn't know her and that was fine, but Wade was his brother and blood was thicker than water. He should be happy for Wade's success. Not resent it.

CeCe clenched her jaw, getting angrier by the second on Wade's behalf and on her own. She was going to enjoy when Wade made the introductions and he figured out who she was.

This guy had no idea who he was dealing with. She'd make him grovel, not just apologize. Then maybe she'd buy this ranch and kick him off the property. Hire guards and ban him forever from the land his grandfather had owned for probably the past sixty years or more.

The more she plotted this man's demise, the harder her heart pounded until she was breathing nearly as heavy as she had been in Wade's bed.

"What'd you get lost?" Wade, shirtless and barefoot and wearing nothing but a pair of cotton shorts, stopped in the doorway. His eyes moved between her and his brother. "I see you two have met."

CeCe decided to take matters into her own hands.

"Not exactly. At least we haven't been properly introduced. I'm CeCe Cole. Owner of Cole Shock Absorbers, though you might recognize me from my modeling career. Of course, that was all before my new occupation as Wade's latest buckle bunny, as you put it." She took a step forward and extended her hand to him, as formally as if she wasn't naked beneath a T-shirt that was far too short. "And your name is?"

He swallowed, sending his Adam's apple bobbing in his throat. "Buck."

"Buck?" Her brows shot up as she glanced at Wade. "Buck Long?"

Wade, lips pressed together as he watched the interaction, nodded. "Yup."

CeCe couldn't help the laugh that erupted from within her. "Oh, that's priceless."

It would make the perfect name for a porn star. That the man was a cowboy made it even more amusing.

Meanwhile, Wade wasn't at all amused, judging by his expression. He turned to his brother. "What did you need, Buck?"

Buck dragged his gaze away from CeCe and concentrated on Wade, while she continued to chuckle at Wade's reminder of his brother's name.

"I, uh, wanted you to know we're planning to move the heifers to the upper pasture tomorrow."

"I'm driving CeCe to the airport tomorrow, late morning. I'll ride up when I get back."

"No need. I'll call the car service I used today." She wasn't about to get blamed for delaying the moving of the heifers, whatever exactly they were. Or be responsible for Wade being blamed for it.

Wade's gaze cut to CeCe. "I'm driving you."

The hardness in his tone told her there was no more room for discussion.

She nodded. "All right. Thank you."

"No problem." Even those words sounded hard. Wade turned to his brother again. "Anything else you need?"

"Nah. That was it."

"A'ight. I'll get back tomorrow as soon as I can."

"Sure. Take your time." Buck's gaze cut to CeCe. "Nice meeting you."

That elicited another snort of a laugh from CeCe. "You too, Buck."

He turned and left through the doorway he'd come through. The sound of the front door of the house clicking shut spurred Wade into action. He strode across the kitchen and brought both hands up to cradle her face.

"CeCe, I don't know what to say. I'm sorry—"

"It's okay."

"No, it's not." His concern was clear and she could see the anger seething inside him.

"Wade, really. I'm fine. I kind of enjoyed putting good old Buck in his place actually."

He let out a breath and she could almost see some of the tension leave his body. The tiniest smile lifted the corner of his mouth. "You did a good job of it too."

"Thank you. But seriously, Wade. Buck Long? Who named him that? Your mother?"

He smiled for real now. "No. He's William after my father. Buck was called Willie until he was a teenager and decided he was too old for that, but it got confusing having two men both named Will in one house."

"So he chose Buck?" she guessed, still amazed.

"No. He earned that nickname riding broncs. He was

165

pretty good too, until he got married and his wife put a stop to it."

Things were beginning to become clearer regarding the tension between the brothers. "That explains a lot."

"Does it?" he asked while looking more interested in pushing her hair back.

He leaned in and brushed kisses from her jawline to her neck, making it hard for her to concentrate on expressing her point. "Yes, it does. He's jealous of your career."

Wade pulled back and laughed. "Yeah, no. I don't think so."

"I do. It was pretty obvious and I only just met him. Just keep that idea in mind. You'll see. His insults and comments about you not being around, they all stem from his being pissed it's not him on that television, traveling the country, picking up all those *buckle bunnies*." She couldn't quell the nausea those two words caused.

CeCe was under no delusions Wade had been a saint before he'd met her, or since, but the thought of those no doubt many women bothered her more than she liked.

"CeCe, Buck is mad because it takes more men than we've got to run this ranch and they could use my help all the time, not just the times I'm home between events." Wade took a step closer, wedging his thigh between hers. "And by the way, I don't seem to have a taste for bunny anymore. I think you might have ruined me in that area. Probably forever."

She couldn't let herself believe words like *forever* when they came out of Wade's mouth. She changed the subject to a safer topic. "Why don't you just hire more men to help out?"

"Life on a ranch is not that simple, city girl." He pressed closer.

CeCe discovered that the two bottles of water currently making her hands wet from the condensation were getting in the way. She was defenseless as Wade ran his hand up her body beneath the T-shirt.

Not that she would have stopped him if she'd had the use of her hands. She wanted him again, as much as ever.

That need scared her. She was leaving tomorrow and they had no plans for when—if—they'd see each other again.

"I got us water," she said, to distract herself from the reality she didn't want to face.

"Great. Bring it to the bedroom with you." He was busy nuzzling her neck and she still had yet to quench the thirst she seemed to have forgotten about.

"Wade?"

"Mmm?"

"Think about what I said about your brother."

"I will. Tomorrow." He pulled back and she saw the desire in his eyes. "Come back to bed."

"Okay."

CHAPTER TWENTY-FIVE

"Sure you can't stay another night?" Wade knew the question was pointless but it was worth a try.

They were at the airport. The pilot had already confirmed that he and the plane were ready when she was. There was no way CeCe would turn around and stay now.

She smiled indulgently. "I've got nothing but the clothes on my back and my purse."

He lifted one shoulder. "So? You looked pretty good in my T-shirt."

"You have work to do. Remember? There are heifers to be moved and . . . other stuff."

His lips twitched at her trying to talk like she knew what she was saying. "Yeah. I remember."

What Wade remembered was the feel of CeCe's hair against his cheek when he woke this morning. And the sound of her losing control when he drove her to heights even he hadn't thought he was capable of last night.

Fuck.

He didn't want her to go but he couldn't expect her to stay. A woman like her had a life to get back to, and like it or not, that life was far from him.

But he could kiss her now while she was still here. Wade intended on doing exactly that and he had no intention of stopping until she made him.

He pressed his mouth to hers and she melted into his kiss.

God, he was going to miss that.

He angled his head and kissed her deeper, plunging his tongue between her lips. The soft moan he heard from her nearly had him crawling out of his clothes.

Making out in front of the airport had its problems. Mainly, airport security knocking on the window. He pulled away from CeCe and glanced at the guard.

"Buddy, you gotta move."

Wade nodded and turned back to CeCe. "I can park the truck in the lot and—"

"No, don't bother. I should go."

With her lips plump from his kisses and her eyes not quite focused, CeCe looked too tempting for Wade to want to let her go, but she was right.

"Okay." Under the watchful eye of the security guard, Wade swung open the driver's side door and then went around to open CeCe's side.

She stepped down from the truck and glanced up at him. "Thanks for the hospitality."

Hospitality. He'd fed her cereal for dinner between rounds of sex. They'd spent most of the time tangled up in his bed. Not knowing when he'd see her again, he had no complaints about that.

He snorted out a short laugh. "Sure. Anytime."

"I'd better head inside." She tipped her head toward the building, but he wasn't ready yet.

Wade grabbed her head one more time and—security guard be damned—kissed her hard and deep.

Finally, somehow, he forced himself to break away. "Let me know when you get home so I know you're safe."

He wanted to hear her voice again, to have some sort of contact, but concern for her safety was the excuse he chose to go with.

"Yes, sir." A smile twitched up her lips.

He yanked his gaze from her too-tempting mouth and dropped his hold on her. "Okay. Safe flight. I—uh—I'll talk to you later."

Damned, if the words *I love you* weren't right there on the tip of his tongue. He felt the blood drain from his face from the shock of that realization.

It had to be because he'd just seen his daughter. Every time they said good-bye it was followed by an *I love you*. Wade decided to go with that theory before he passed out from shock and fear that he might be in love with a woman he had no future with.

"Talk to you later." Oblivious to the drama playing out inside Wade, CeCe treated him to a tiny smile and turned toward the building.

He stood and waited until she was through the door. Then he waited longer until he couldn't see her inside through the glass, all while knowing he was pushing his luck with the guard.

His wait had been worth it. She'd turned and glanced back at him, wiggling her fingers in a small wave before she disappeared. He lifted his hand to return her gesture but she was already gone.

Her backward glance had his throat tightening. He forced himself to turn around and get in the truck before he lost all sense and ran after her.

Fuck. He needed a drink.

Instead, he drove back to the ranch. He didn't dare stop by his house where the memories of CeCe were everywhere. He drove directly to the barn and parked.

Wade had just swung the barn door open when his grandfather pulled up behind him.

When the old man had made his way out of the truck and over to him, Wade said, "Hey, Gramps."

The older man nodded. "Mornin'."

His grandfather didn't mention the lateness of the hour or the fact Wade was just now pulling in for work.

It wasn't quite noon yet so technically it was still morning, but Wade still felt the guilt of his late arrival. Because of that, he needed to get right to work. He moved inside the barn and toward the saddle racks as his grandfather followed.

Wade pulled his saddle off the rack on the wall and carried it to the stall where a Paint Quarterhorse watched him without much enthusiasm.

"So Buck says you got a super model stashed away at your place. That true?"

The question had Wade pausing. He had no choice but to answer. "It was."

"Really?" His grandfather lifted one bushy gray eyebrow.

His grandfather was not an easy man to impress but he obviously was now. That's what it took to impress the old man? A supermodel?

Wade had to laugh. "Yup. But don't get too excited about it. I just dropped her off at the airport. At her private jet." He threw that last tidbit in knowing it was over the top but enjoying his grandfather's reaction anyway.

"Where the hell you meet her?"

"The Cole Shock Absorbers Invitational in California a couple weeks ago. She's CeCe Cole."

The old man's eyes widened more. "You better marry that girl before she gets away."

Wade let out a snort. "Yeah, because my first attempt at marriage went so well."

And that was just one of the many reasons why the suggestion was ridiculous.

The old man adjusted the faded *U.S. Navy Veteran* baseball hat on his head. "When life gives you a reride, boy, you take it. Keep your eye on the road ahead, not in the rearview worrying about what's behind you."

His grandfather was chock full of philosophy today.

Wade didn't argue, even if he did think the words were just that. Words. "I'll remember that. So, I better saddle up and get out there before Dad and Buck get any more pissed I missed half a day of work."

CAT JOHNSON

"I was about to jump on the four wheeler and ride out myself. I got some news. Maybe if you deliver it, they'll forget about you getting here late."

Doubtful. "Sure. What's the news?"

"I got an interesting call just now. From some cowboy relief fund. They supposedly help out guys hurt while rodeoing."

The mention of the organization—the one CeCe had just begun to sponsor—caught Wade's attention. "Yeah. I know of 'em. What'd they have to say?"

"Apparently the ranch qualifies for some sort of grant for a work program they got."

"We do?" Wade gave up on saddling the horse and turned his full attention to his grandfather.

"Yup. This woman, Parks, I think her name was, was a little sketchy on the details but from what I can figure, they're sending over a guy for us to try out. If we like him, he'll work here as many hours as he can handle and this organization will pay him."

This sounded too convoluted to be true, until Wade took into account his conversation with CeCe last night. Her solution to his family trouble was to just hire more help. It was too much of a coincidence that hot on the heels of that talk with her, this offer comes through from the very organization she'd recently written a no doubt sizeable check to.

His grandfather continued, "So we get free labor. He gets a job to help get him back on his feet financially after his injury. Seems like a win-win to me."

"Yup. It sure does." Wade had no proof CeCe had any hand in this but damned if it didn't seem like it.

If she did have a hand in this, when the hell had she accomplished it? He'd been with her all night and all morning.

Then again, she was the owner of a huge corporation with a company full of employees dedicated to doing her bidding. One phone call and she could have any number of staff

172

working on it.

All because he'd mentioned they needed more hands to help out on the ranch.

The woman never failed to surprise him. As if he hadn't liked her too much already, now he liked her even more, just when he feared he was already veering into territory well past *like.*

Loving CeCe Cole was the dead last thing he should do, no matter what his grandfather said. Wade knew first hand that more often than not taking that reride just got you thrown in the dirt with no score on the board.

He made short work of saddling the horse and turned to his grandfather. "I'm gonna head out."

The old man tipped his head. "Don't forget to tell them the news. The guy is coming first thing in the morning."

"A'ight." With a lot more on his mind than any man should while on the back of a horse and surrounded by thousands of acres Wade headed out at a gallop.

He found his brother and father easily enough. Not that they were going to make things easy on him.

His father made a point of glancing at his watch before saying, "Wade."

"Dad."

The older man glanced at the horizon. "There's a group of stragglers over past the ridge. You two go round them up."

"Yes, sir." Wade drew in a breath to brace himself for the shit Buck would surely give him the moment they were alone.

"So, your supermodel fly away home?"

And there it was.

The last thing Wade wanted to do was answer Buck's question but he had no choice. "Yup."

Buck let out a snort. "I'm surprised you didn't go with her."

"For one, I promised I'd be home during this break."

"Pfft, you've broken that promise before."

Wade grit his teeth but didn't argue the point given he'd spent nearly a week with CeCe in California rather than come home. "The truth is she lives in her world and I live in another."

A world where the herd had to get moved, though it seemed Buck was more concerned with Wade's personal life.

Buck snorted. "Hell, Wade, if you think that's true, then you've taken one too many shots to the head. You've had at least one foot in her world—that greedy corporate world—for years now."

Wade scowled at his brother. "I do not."

"No? Then how come I can't turn on the TV without seeing you, larger than life on that damn giant screened television my wife insisted on buying? You getting interviewed by the reporters. You wearing the Cole name all over your jersey. You holding that energy drink up to the camera and grinning for all the world to see, acting as if it didn't taste like shit just because they pay you to."

"For what the sponsors contribute to the circuit for no guaranteed ROI, that's the least I can do."

His brother's eyes popped wide. "ROI? Can you hear yourself, Wade? That's exactly what I mean. You're more CeCe Cole's people than ours nowadays."

His brother's words were meant to wound but all they did was point to a truth Wade hadn't fully realized until this moment. He was straddling two worlds, and had been for a while.

It was no wonder he felt so stretched half the time.

More importantly, maybe it wasn't so out of the question for him to make it in CeCe's world.

CHAPTER TWENTY-SIX

CeCe stared out the window of the plane that was taking her away from Texas and Wade.

The ringing of the phone interrupted her misery. Glancing at the unfamiliar number on the screen, she missed the days when there were no phones on planes and a person had a few hours of peace and quiet.

Those days were over. Sighing, she answered, "Hello?"

"Mrs. Cole? It's Verna Parks."

From the rider charity. This call, CeCe was happy to take. "Ms. Parks, it's good to hear from you so soon. Did everything work out?"

"It did indeed. The ranch was surprised but really happy to be part of your idea. And of course, the gentleman we put up for the job is very grateful."

"Good. I'm glad to hear it all worked out." At least something good would come out of her trip to Texas. Besides her getting more attached to the man she'd left behind. "You didn't mention my name, correct?"

"Correct. We handled it just as you requested."

"Thank you. I appreciate it."

"Of course. It was a very generous thing to do and

wanting to do it anonymously, it's just amazing."

Not so amazing. Paying a man to work for a year on a ranch cost less than her last vacation with John had. "Thanks for keeping me updated."

"My pleasure. Have a good day, Mrs. Cole and thank you again."

"You're welcome." CeCe disconnected the call but didn't put down the phone.

Instead she dialed Dr. Stein's number. The one for his cell phone. She'd long since stopped going through his receptionist. Yet another perk of the wealthy.

"Hello, CeCe."

"Hello, doctor. Um, is this a bad time?"

"Not at all. I'm in the car driving but I can talk if you need to. Is everything okay?"

"Yes. That's the problem."

"Would you like to elaborate?"

"I spent the night with Wade and it was perfect." Or near perfect except for the intrusion of his brother. And even that had only given her more insight into what was behind Wade as a man.

"And you feel that's a problem because?"

"Because I like him. A lot." CeCe more than liked him.

If she let herself, she'd fall head over heels for Wade. Too fast. Too hard. Then she'd crash and burn when it ended.

On the other end of the phone the doctor was silent.

"Doctor? Are you there?"

"I'm here." He drew in an audible breath. "CeCe . . ."

His tone wasn't encouraging. She wasn't going to like what he was going to say. She felt it to her bones.

"To anyone who's gone through a major life change, such as a divorce, I recommend they take time to get used to their new life before starting a new relationship. But for you, with your propensity for jumping into relationships too fast, I think that advice is doubly important."

"So you're saying . . . what?"

"That you need to be alone for a little while. Get

comfortable with yourself. Learn to love yourself before you try to love someone else."

She tried to take a deep breath but her chest felt too tight. "How long?"

"A year at minimum. Ideally, I'd recommend two years."

Two years alone? Even one year sounded like an eternity.

"CeCe, I can only give my advice. I can't make you take it. But if you want to heal and grow and to break out of this cycle of dependency on others that you've been living with basically your entire life, I strongly suggest you do as I suggested."

"Okay."

"I'm going to have to hang up. Are you going to be all right?"

"Yes. I'm perfect. You've given me a lot to think of. Thank you."

"You're very welcome. I'll see you next week for our regular appointment?"

"Yes. Good bye, doctor." CeCe disconnected the call and stared at the phone.

A year of no contact with Wade. By then he'd have forgotten all about her and moved on to the next woman he picked up at the rodeo.

It was probably for the best. If she ignored the doctor and pursued anything more with Wade she'd get clingy like she always did. He'd get tired of it and her. Then she'd be alone again anyway.

Best to cut her losses early this time before she got in any deeper.

The problem was, she was already in too deep.

CHAPTER TWENTY-SEVEN

"And the crowd has really gathered here today for the Salt Lake City, Utah event. After being off for a couple of weeks, the contenders in the race for the number one slot should be well rested and ready to go. Only five hundred points separate the number one and number two riders in the standings . . . "

Wade only half listened to the announcer's amplified ramblings as he stretched behind the chutes.

He wasn't as young as he used to be. To be quick and limber required he stretch. Even if stretching didn't help, it certainly couldn't hurt. A pulled groin muscle could take a man out—in so many ways.

Thinking of those ways inevitably brought Wade's thoughts back to CeCe. Not that that was anything new. The damn woman was on his mind day and night.

Even if he had been able to forget about her, the damn red hairs he kept finding everywhere would remind him.

CeCe's hair was in his truck clinging to the back of the passenger seat. In his bathroom at home. Even inside his suitcase—he'd found one on his T-shirt that she'd worn for barely an hour when she'd gone to the kitchen.

Each and every time he discovered one of the long strands sent him into a tailspin. He'd find himself smiling at the reminder even as his gut twisted from missing her.

Hell, once he even almost teared up.

"Aaron, we're in Salt Lake City, for God's sake. Relax. Why would CeCe Cole be here?" Garret James's voice behind him traveled down Wade's spine like the sound of nails on a chalkboard.

"Because she's crazy?" Chase suggested.

"Or just obsessed with Aaron because he showed her such good loving for those two nights."

Wade spun around in time to see Garret grinning wide. A grin Wade would like to knock off the cocky kid's face.

The three stood by the chutes, working the resin into their ropes in preparation for their rides.

His blood pressure high thanks to their conversation, Wade strode toward the group.

"Hey, Wade. How you—"

Wade cut off Chase's greeting. "I haven't said anything before but I gotta say it now. You guys need to quit mouthing off and talking shit about Ms. Cole."

The color draining from Chase's face as Wade laid into them provided some satisfaction. It was quickly wiped away by Garret's snort. "If you knew some of the crazy shit—"

Wade spun on Garret. "I don't give a shit what she did or said. You start showing some respect for the woman who bears the name that paid for this event you're riding in tonight. This is a small world we work in. Too small to be talking shit about anyone, but especially about a woman who's been through what she has this past year. You got it?"

Aaron shot a glance at Garret and answered, "Yes, sir."

Wade nodded. "Good."

Still pissed, he pivoted and got the hell away from them before he said anything else to the kids.

Somewhere in the back of his mind he realized he was as pissed that he hadn't heard from CeCe since he'd seen her in Texas, as he was mad at the kids for talking shit.

He'd been making an effort to get back to work, back to normal, seeing if he could survive without even the hope of CeCe in his life. Now the answer was clear.

~ * ~

"What are you doing?"

Maria glanced up from the kitchen counter. "Cooking dinner, Mrs. Cole. Am I doing something wrong?"

The woman thought she was in trouble, just because CeCe was in the kitchen questioning her. That just proved that CeCe usually didn't do either—go into the room or bother to wonder what Maria was doing there.

"No, nothing is wrong." She took a step closer. "What are you making?"

"Spinach salad with this on top." Maria held up the plate with a thick, beautiful piece of raw Ahi tuna on it. It was one of CeCe's favorite dinners.

The ingredients laid out in front Maria looked simple enough, yet CeCe wouldn't have any clue how to go about making the meal even with as many times as she'd eaten it.

Maybe she could watch Maria prepare the meal and learn . . . and maybe not. One look at Maria's face told CeCe the housekeeper would rather have her boss anywhere else besides the kitchen overseeing her preparations.

"Looks good." CeCe turned and left the woman to it before she had a stroke from nerves.

She'd have to take a cooking class if she wanted to learn. That might be fun actually. And it would get her out of the house for a night or two a week. This self imposed ban on men and relationships had CeCe climbing the walls.

How many miles could a woman run or bike in the gym?

It hadn't even been two weeks yet since the doctor's decree and already she had cabin fever. A person wasn't supposed to get that during the summer in California.

Of course, it had nothing to do with the weather and everything to do with the fact she wouldn't let herself call or text Wade.

That didn't stop her from thinking about him. Or craving him.

Her handheld shower massager had never gotten so much use. The doctor hadn't said she couldn't do *that*. Not that she'd specifically asked him. There were some subjects even she wasn't willing to broach in therapy.

The sound of the doorbell had CeCe frowning. She didn't generally get unplanned visitors. Especially now that John no longer lived in the house.

She heard Maria's footsteps headed her way, but CeCe was already by the front door. "I'll get it, Maria."

"Yes, ma'am."

CeCe pulled open the heavy door and felt her heart stop. "Wade."

A small smile tipped up his lips. "Hey, beautiful."

God, how she'd missed hearing his voice. She couldn't count how many people had called her beautiful throughout her lifetime, but hearing it from Wade's lips had an effect on her she couldn't explain.

"Hi." Her voice sounded breathless. "I didn't know you were coming."

He snorted out a laugh. "Neither did I. I had an event so I decided to stop by after."

"An event here in California?" She'd been trying to keep off the internet to avoid the temptation of searching for Wade's schedule.

"It wasn't exactly in California." He looked uncomfortable, avoiding eye contact before he finally brought his gaze up to meet hers. "It was in Utah."

She widened her eyes. "Utah? That's far."

And California wasn't even close to being on his way home to Texas.

"Eh, not too bad. Besides, it seems we have some new help working at the ranch so I didn't have to rush back." He lifted one brow. "You happen to know anything about that?"

"Maybe." She felt the blood rush to her cheeks even as

she realized they were still standing in the doorway. "Come on in."

Inviting him inside would hopefully make him forget the topic of conversation—her sneaking around behind his back and hiring help for his ranch.

Wade wasted no time coming in, not even waiting for her to clear the path. He pushed the door closed as he backed CeCe against the wall of the foyer.

She'd taken her shoes off after work and had to look up to see him as he towered over her. She saw the desire in his eyes as he lowered his head before claiming her mouth with a kiss.

It started out soft and got more thorough as Wade angled his head and stroked his tongue against hers.

She'd missed this with him too.

CeCe heard footsteps and the telltale gasp that had become a familiar occurrence whenever Wade was around and Maria was working. "Mrs. Cole. I'm sorry. Mr. Wade. You're back."

Hands braced against the wall, Wade pulled back enough to turn his head and smile at the housekeeper. "Hey, Maria. You're looking lovely tonight."

"Thank you, Mr. Wade." The older woman's cheeks flushed at his compliment.

"Mrs. Cole, will Mr. Wade be staying for dinner?"

CeCe raised her gaze to Wade. "Will he?"

"Maria, can you put a hold on that dinner for, I don't know, about an hour, hour and a half?"

"Yes, sir."

"Then I reckon I'll stay." He pushed off the wall and grabbed CeCe's hand.

"Where are we going?" CeCe asked as he pulled her across the foyer.

"You really have to ask?"

No. The heated glance he sent her answered the question for him.

Inside her bedroom, Wade closed the door. But he didn't take her to the bed. He didn't tear off her clothes or his own.

Instead he sat on the wing chair by the window and pulled her into his lap.

"Chair sex?" she asked. She eyed the high arms and back. "That might be tough."

"We're not having sex."

"We're not?" Her voice rose high with surprise.

The corner of Wade's mouth tipped up. "A'ight. We are, but not right this minute."

That was more like the Wade she knew.

"Then what are we doing, right this minute?"

Making out would be good. She already felt like a damned teenager around him. She might as well act like one too.

"We're going to talk."

"Okay. About?"

"Us."

Her heart thundered. "Us?"

The doctor's words niggled at the back of her brain. He'd said she shouldn't be an *us* at least for a year, maybe two. She'd only made it two weeks. Not two years.

But to be fair, she hadn't pursued this relationship and she wasn't the one to bring up the subject now. She'd been good and followed orders. As much as it had killed her to do it, she hadn't even texted Wade to tell him she'd landed safely.

The whole time CeCe had been holding the internal debate with herself and the echo of her doctor's words in her own head, Wade had looked as if he was in pain.

Oh, God. She was so stupid. Maybe he wanted to make it clear to her that they would never be anything more than sex so she didn't get confused by his long distance booty call.

She turned her full attention to him. Delaying the inevitable wouldn't solve anything.

"Wade, what do you want to say?"

"This—you and me—it isn't just about sex for me. Not anymore."

Her eyes widened. "Then what is this between you and me?"

"Hell if I know." He drew in a breath. "But I'm pretty sure

I'm having . . . feelings."

His expression when he said the word—feelings—was so telling CeCe had to hide her smile. It was as if he was shocked and appalled at the mere fact he had them. As if the word tasted bad in his mouth.

"And these feelings, can you put a name to them perhaps?" She bit her lip and waited, her own feelings soaring.

Obviously unhappy she'd pressed him further, he pulled his mouth to one side. Finally, he huffed out a breath.

He was having trouble maintaining eye contact as he said, "I think I probably love you. I know. I don't near deserve you. Tell me to get the hell out and I'll understand."

She cupped his face in her hands, forcing him to look at her. "I'm the one who doesn't deserve you."

He rolled his eyes. "Yeah, right."

"Shut up and kiss me." She leaned in but before she pressed her mouth to his, she repeated his words back to him. "And I think I probably love you too."

He let out a breath, his relief visible before he crashed into her mouth. Before she knew what had happened, Wade had stood with her in his arms and they were tumbling onto her bed.

"Now we're having sex." He grinned.

"I figured that."

Wade sobered as he braced over her. "I'm not gonna lie to you. I have no idea how to go about making this thing work between me and you. All I know is I'm willing to do whatever it takes. I hope that's good enough."

"Yes. That's good enough. And you know, I was thinking how I wouldn't mind spending some more time in Texas."

His eyes flew wide. "Would you?"

"I would. If you wanted me to."

"Hell yeah, I want you to." His eyes narrowed. "Don't you know I always want you? Day and night. When I'm trying to work. When I'm trying to sleep. All I can think about is you."

"Good." She smiled.

"Yeah, I figured you'd like hearing that." He shook his head but his amusement was soon replaced by his concentration as he focused on her pencil skirt. "I'm liking this sexy secretary look."

"Secretary?" She lifted a brow. "Sexy *CEO*, thank you."

"Fine." He grinned. "Now let's make you a sexy naked CEO."

"Only if you'll be my naked cowboy."

"A bit of a stretch but I think I can make it work." He ran his hands down her body, over her clothes as he straddled her. "God, I missed you."

"I missed you too." More than she'd been willing to admit even to herself.

His gaze hit on her bedside table and the drawer filled with lube and toys. He shook his head. "I'm so crazy about you, I might even let you do to me what you were trying."

She had to control a surprised laugh. "Wow, that is crazy."

"I know. That's what I'm saying. You make me insane." He leaned low and spoke close enough he could kiss her in between his sentences. "You make me want to be things I'm not. Do things I never wanted to do."

Wade shook his head, once again looking baffled at the whole situation.

Being in love was obviously a new thing for him.

She fell in love too fast and Wade not at all—complete opposites, the two of them made a hell of a pair. But maybe that was a good thing.

Two halves of one whole. Yin and yang. They'd complement each other. Like a partnership. CeCe liked the idea of that.

Almost giddy with anticipation, she reached up and stroked the stubble on his cheeks. "It's okay, baby. I'll be gentle."

Wade let out a sigh. "Yup. Completely insane."

"Mmm, hmm." She nodded. "I love you though."

"That's damn good because I'm completely in love with you." He drew in and blew out a long slow breath.

For a moment, he looked a little pale in spite of his tan and she seriously feared he might pass out.

"Wow. This love stuff is completely out of my wheelhouse." After swallowing hard, Wade brought his gaze up to meet hers. "Can we fuck now, please? At least I'm good at that."

As far as CeCe was concerned, Wade was pretty good at the love stuff too, in spite of the fact it obviously scared the hell out of him.

She smiled at his discomfort and teased, "Yes, my golden-tongued poet, we can fuck now."

His eyes widened as he laughed. "I'll show you golden-tongued."

He slid down her body while pushing up her skirt and CeCe was very glad he'd told Maria to hold dinner. This could take awhile.

If you enjoyed Wrecked, *don't miss the rest of the Studs in Spurs series! And please consider leaving a review.*

ABOUT THE AUTHOR

A *New York Times* & *USA Today* bestselling author, Cat Johnson writes contemporary romance featuring sexy alpha heroes, men in uniform, and cowboys. Known for her unique marketing and research practices, she has sponsored pro bull riders, owns a collection of camouflage and western wear for book signings, and a fair number of her friends/book consultants wear combat or cowboy boots for a living. She writes both full length and shorter works.

For more visit CatJohnson.net
Join the mailing list at catjohnson.net/news

Printed in Great Britain
by Amazon